Lovers

love and sex stories

tee corinne

BB

BANNED BOOKS
Austin, Texas

A Banned Book

FIRST EDITION

Copyright ©1989
By Tee A. Corinne

Published in the United States of America
By Edward-William Publishing Company
Number 231, P.O. Box 33280, Austin, Texas 78764

ISBN 0-934411-17-4

Some of these stories first appeared in On Our Backs and Yoni.

Dedicated to Beverly Brown, with appreciation.

Acknowledgments

I want to thank Tangren Alexander and the members of the Southern Oregon Women Writer's Group; Gourmet Eating Society and Chorus; Con Sellers; Georgia Cole; Bill Doody; Susie Bright, editor of *On Our Backs*; and Beee Langley, editor of *Yoni*; for the many ways they contributed to this book's growth and form. A very special thank you goes to Lee Lynch for her care and support.

Contents

also by Tee Corinne:

- *Dreams of the Woman Who Loved Sex*
- *Yantras of Womanlove*
- *Women Who Loved Women*, an illustrated bibliography
- *The Cunt Coloring Book* (also published as *Labiaflowers*)
- *The Southern Oregon Women Writers' Group, Gourmet Eating Society and Chorus Picture Book*
- *Drawings '83*
- *Joy Unfolds*
- *Cream*

Introduction

Erotica can stimulate the mind as well as the body, illuminate sexuality, and validate shared experiences. Lesbians in the U.S. have been producing erotica since 1975, the publication date of *What Lesbians Do* and of *Loving Women*. Both books radically, lovingly pushed forward verbal and visual boundaries, changing the nature of woman-identified sexual discourse.

This book, *Lovers*, grew out of my interest in the function of erotic writing; in how we, as lesbians, explore sexual issues, learn to grow within long-term relationships, share with new lovers, and use sexual energy as a healing force in our lives.

A Language In Which To Love

As lesbians, our sexuality binds us together. It creates ties of friendship between former lovers and electrical connections between would be, present, and future lovers. It is not irrelevant. It is central. And until recently, we have been very silent about it.

Naming, having words for the experiences of our lives, is an essential ingredient of sanity, of the ability to pass our experiences and our culture, on to future generations.

Marilyn Frye, in the germinal essay *Lesbian "Sex"* talks about the effects of sexual silence:

"Most of my lifetime, most of my experience in the realms commonly designated as 'sexual' has been pre-linguistic, non-cognitive. I have, in effect, no linguistic community, no language, and therefore in one important sense, no knowledge." Later she says that "... The meanings one's life and experience might generate cannot come fully into operation if they are not woven into language."

Women's sexuality in general and lesbian sexuality within it, have, until recently had a fairly circumscribed and limited vocabulary. That is changing for those of us with access to women's bookstores and media, with books like *Lesbian Bedtime Stories* and *The Leading Edge* (lesbian); *Pleasures, Erotic Interludes, and Herotica* (mixed proclivities); *Ladies Own Erotica* (heterosex) and Califia's *Macho Sluts* for lesbians interested in s/m.

The best of the new sex writing paints a broad picture of how we can be sexual with ourselves and with each other. It also offers new ways to understand the nature of libido.

Physical, Mental, Psychic and Transformative Sex

Judy Grahn weaves a multi-dimensional sexuality and sexual language throughout *Another Mother Tongue* with a concentration in chapter nine, "Friction Among Women": "But we secret Lesbians were keenly aware of the real fire between us, the friction that warms." In this chapter Grahn defines the realms of erotic power as: physical, mental, psychic and transformative. Magically, she moves from one to another, naming, explaining and enabling.

Of the world of the senses (which is the level on which most erotica initially focuses) Grahn says:

" The first domain is the physical, the basic flesh-to-flesh contact of sexual relationship. It is based in touch, sensation, smell, intense feelings, intimacy, sharing. In the first domain a Lesbian learns to receive sexual love from

2

another woman, to trust her vulva to a stranger's hands and lips and tongue, to be able to let go and come in her presence, in her very face."

Grahn draws together a complex net of ideas, offering the reader a new understanding of fantasy, power and creativity and their potential for changing the world.

It seems to me that French Canadian writer Nicole Brossard gives voice and form to a multi-layered sexuality in works like *Sous La Langue* (Under Tongue):

"You cannot foresee so suddenly leaning towards a face and wanting to lick the soul's whole body till the gaze sparks with furies and yieldings. You cannot foresee the body's being swept into the infinity of curves, of pulsings, every time the body surges you cannot see the images, the hand touching the nape of the neck, the tongue parting the hairs, the knees trembling, the arms from such desire encircling the body like a universe."

Creating Words

The words we choose to use for sex, once we have them, change and grow with our moods, our inclinations, the intensity of our desire. I've always liked the term "handcrafting" for manual stimulation, but there are times when "finger-fucking" is the precise concept I want to convey, to hold onto and move into. Recently I've come to favor the word "mating" for its combined meaning of sexual union and psychological bonding, the making of "mates."

Dicey Yates (pseudonym) in *Mystical Unioning*, uses special terms like sexlove, womon/womon unioning and mutual transcendency when talking of ways to move deeper into the sexual experience. Isabel Miller in *Patience and Sarah* called orgasm "melting," a word with both visceral and psychic connotations.

Jacqueline Lapidus, among others, uses the French term 'cyprine' for female sexual secretions. Brossard and her translator suggest 'cyprin' for English usage.

Yvonne Eldresse, in *Lesbia Lyrics*, mates words in order to expand their usefulness as in "wild womonmouth," "ladyfingers" and "honeycunt."

Cassandra employs a playful use of language in *Scent of Femme Fatale*: "Her parfumnatural erotique/ an exotique veil that covers head to toe . . ." to convey the excitement and joy of loving, of an exuberant sexuality.

The New Sex Writing

Overtly sexy passages appear more frequently than they used to in lesbian romances. This began with the deservedly popular sex scene in *Curious Wine* in which the word "breast" is the only specific anatomical notation and includes Lee Lynch's "Dusty Eats Out" with its memorable first line: " 'Dusty, Lover?' Elly asked. 'Aren't you ever going to go down on me?' "

In *Dead Heat*, a thriller, Willyce Kim melds poetry with lust and charm:

"Frankie Tucker moaned and spread Cody's legs apart. She slowly tongued petals and ridges and greatmother-of-pearl. Cody Roberts flung her arms over her head and arched herself into Frankie's mouth. The room spinning around them filled with Cody's coming. In the moonlight, with sweat dancing off their bodies, Frankie Tucker moved slowly over Cody's heaving limbs."

And in *Trash* Dorothy Allison crafts from her own life powerful erotic passages that defy circumspect parameters:

"I preferred the women I brought home from the pool hall, the ones who liked me biting them, liked biting me, liked whispering dirty words, wrestling, and shoving their calloused fingers between my labia until I bit them harder and harder, my mouth full of the taste of them, the texture of their skin, their smoky, powerful smell, soaking them up, swallowing and swallowing. Making love with them I rise right up out of myself. I'm happy then in a way I never seem to be otherwise, sure of myself and not afraid. I lose all my self-consciousness, my fear of saying or doing the wrong thing."

4

Texas '52 by Stephanie (C.S.) Henderson carries the reader along with a driving beat, with a compelling need:

". . . Then you pulled me to you, and I started gigglin'—and makin' love that night was a place just short of Heaven—wasn't nothin' ever good as you that night—the moon got bigger and brighter and filled the whole sky. That moon was as big as Texas itself, the moon was a Goddess lookin' down at us, laughin'—pleased at our gift of sweat and come—and when we screamed . . .

"I ain't never felt a scream like that. That scream started at the base of my spine, crackled up to my shoulders and spread down my arms, and I thought I was hurtin' you I was squeezin' so hard—and you was cryin'; I was cryin'—bodies shakin' like with the DT's. That scream cut through that prairie night and swallowed it." (Yoni/Summer 1987)

In the delightful story "Tortilleras," Terri de la Peña tempts us with flirtation, with the minute transitions of courtship: "Veronica studied her, liking the way Talamantes had pronounced her name in perfect Spanish—Veh-roe-nee-ka—a verbal caress."

Jess Wells in *The Dress* fetishizes and almost comes over a bit of thrift store finery: "It zips. To the top. And it's incredible, because that slinky material is lying in folds across my ass and I can feel the air rushing up to my cunt." (*The Dress, The Cry And A Shirt With No Seams*)

In "The Love Making" Cenen uses an exuberance of language to evoke the physicality of sex:

"When the swell of your clitoris came bulging into the roll of my sucking tongue, I knew tonight's sweetness would be long. My excited body moved closer into the swelling folds of your labia, rubbing my teeth, my lips, my whole face into your wetness. Your body jumped and turned spasmodically pressing my heat between your legs." (Compañeras: Latina Lesbians)

Doing It Ourselves

Often we write to excite ourselves and our lovers, then get published or self-publish in order to broaden the communication, spread the energy around. Midgett in *Brown On Brown, Black Lesbian Erotica* writes "She starts to rub my ass and I can feel the tears coming again, 'Oh brown womyn' I whispered, 'Oh brown womyn, fuck me, fuck me . . .' "

Wanda Honn strings a sequence of explicit episodes together in *Rapture*. In one story a waitress tells the narrator to meet her downstairs by the bathroom. ". . . my waitress nudged me slightly forward and we both slipped into the stall. I laughed uneasily, turning to face her, and she kissed me hard and passionately. Then, while tonguing my ear, she whispered, 'I'm sorry this will have to be quick; I don't have much time.' "

Let It Begin With Our Lives

Susie Bright, editor of *On Our Backs*, has said that erotica is about escapism. Yet the true story, honestly written, holds a potential for opening deep levels of excitement, levels that can easily be integrated into our everyday lives. Sherry Thomas, writing as Jennifer Snow, created just such a piece in "All We Really Are is Open" from *Country Women's* sexuality issue. In a candid first person narrative she writes about initial contact, fears, forcing orgasm, and a range of sometimes taboo activities such as making love with your whole hand inside a lovers vagina and of anal stimulation.

"She touched my anus with her finger. 'It's just another hole, you know,' she said. One night, three fingers inside her vagina, pushing deeply, deeply, my fourth went in her anus, pushing deeply. I felt an anguishing, tearing kind of pleasure run all through me. Forbidden territory; deeper union. Desire and love were all confused within me. I wanted her. I wanted her to know more pleasure than she ever had. My thumb rubbed her clitoris too. 'Oh honey, honey, baby!' she cried out."

Thomas also talks about the need for words:

" 'I wish we had a language,' I said, 'we are so awkward when we talk. You say 'eat me'; I say 'kiss my cunt' —neither is right. 'Cunt' is a man's word; 'vagina' and 'clitoris' are so clinical; 'eat me' and 'touch me' seem embarrassed into generalities; I want a language to love you in.' "

Fantasy Food and Sex For the Mind

From the density and complex levels of caring in Joan Nestle's *Esther* (A Restricted Country) to the structured sex education of JoAnn Loulan's *Lesbian Sex* and Pat Califia's *Sapphistry*, lesbians are making language and meaning work together to facilitate a literature the likes of which has never existed before.

Within this growing cornucopia, it's interesting to notice that the discreetly handled sex scenes in Ann Bannon's novels are still a turn on and the erotic passages from Gale Wilhelm's books still glow in my memory.

The ability of something to live in memory, to be held onto by one's mind, seems to me especially important in sexuality where recall often integrates with experience to create arousal. It is at the level of mental excitement that the new writing most challenges us, offering material to discuss, dream into and of course, take to bed.

Into this matrix I offer you *Lovers*, twenty stories about sexuality. As you read it, know that I'm wishing you hours of entertainment, thought provoking diversions, and perhaps a notion or two, to be explored on a leisurely afternoon or a long winter's night.

Bibliography

Dorothy Allison, *Trash* (Ithaca, NY: Firebrand Books, 1988).

———, "Demon Lover," *On Our Backs*, vol. 5, #1 (San Francisco, CA, 1988).

Lonnie Barbach, ed., *Pleasures, Women Write Erotica* (Garden City, NY: Doubleday, 1984).

———, ed., *Erotic Interludes, Tales Told By Women* (Garden city, NY: Doubleday, 1986).

Susie Bright, "Surveying Contemporary Lesbian Erotica," Lambda Rising Book Report (Washington, D.C., 1988).

———, ed., *Herotica* (Burlingame, CA: Down There Press, 1988).

Nicole Brossard, *Sous La Langue/Under Tongue*, trans. by Susanne de Lotbinière-Harwood (Montreal, Quebec, Canada: L'Essentielle, èditrices/Gynergy Books).

Pat Califia, *Macho Sluts* (Boston, MA: Alyson, 1988).

———, *Sapphistry* (Tallahassee, FL: Naiad Press, 1980).

Cassandra, "Scent of Femme Fatale," Common Lives/Lesbian Lives #26 (Iowa City, IA, 1988).

Cenen, "The Love Making," *Compañeras: Latina Lesbians* (New York, NY: Latina Lesbian History Project, 1987).

Terri de la Peña, "Tortilleras," *Lesbian Bedtime Stories* (Little River, CA: Tough Dove Books, 1989).

Yvonne Eldresse, *Lesbia Lyrics* (Seattle, WA: Eldresse Press, 1988).

Katherine W. Forrest, *Curious Wine* (Tallahassee, FL: Naiad Press, 1983).

Marilyn Frye, "Lesbian 'Sex'," Sinister Wisdom #36 (Berkeley CA, 1988).

Marilyn Gayle and Barbary Katherine, *What Lesbians Do* (Portland, OR: Godiva, 1975).

Judy Grahn, *Another Mother Tongue* (Boston, MA: Beacon Press, 1984).

Stephanie (C.S.) Henderson, "Texas '52," Yoni, Summer 1987 (Oakland, CA).

Wanda Honn, *Rapture* (Brooklyn, NY: A Wanda Honn Publication, 1987).

Willyce Kim, *Dead Heat* (Boston, MA: Alyson, 1988).

Jacqueline Lapidus, "Design for the City of Women," *Sailing The Road Clear #6* (Old Mystic, CT, 1978) and *Yantras Of Womanlove* (Tallahassee, FL: Naiad Press 1982).

JoAnn Loulan, *Lesbian Sex* (San Francisco, CA: Spinsters Ink, 1984).

———, *Lesbian Passion* (San Francisco, CA: Spinsters/Aunt Lute, 1987).

Lee Lynch, "From a Novel in Progress: Dusty Eats Out," *Home In Your Hands* (Tallahassee, FL: Naiad Press, 1986).

Midgett, *Brown On Brown, Black Lesbian Erotica* (San Francisco, CA, 1987).

Joan Nestle, *A Restricted Country* (Ithaca, NY: Firebrand Books, 1987).

———, "Writing About Sex," Bad Attitude, A Lesbian Sex Magazine (Cambridge, MA, 1987).

The Nomadic Sisters, *Loving Women* (Sonora, CA, 1975).

Sherry Thomas, "All we really are is open," Country Women, sexuality issue (Albion, CA, 1975).

Dicey Yates, "Mystical Unioning," Lesbian Ethics vol. 2, #3 (Venice, CA, 1987).

Lady Winston, ed., *The Leading Edge* (Denver, CO: Lace Publications, 1987).

Jess Wells, *The Dress, The Cry And A Shirt With No Seams* (Oakland, CA, n.d.).

Terry Woodrow, ed., *Lesbian Bedtime Stories* (Little River, CA: Tough Dove Books, 1989).

Spring Blossoms

Spring was a feast this year: waxy snowdrops first and violets, pink and white and many purples, then yellow daffodils and small translucent white ones and creamy ones with egg-yoke yellow centers. Tiny spring beauties sprouted near the mailbox, vinca minor turned their small cobalt faces up from rich greenery. Flowering quince exploded overnight into labia-orange rays.

I reached for you in the morning, every morning, feeling myself flowering too, my own sap rising and spilling over into an excess of energy, of passion, of sheer exuberant good spirits.

Sometimes you responded. Sometimes you nuzzled and went back to sleep. Sometimes I masturbated there in bed beside you, then you'd come wide awake, helping, rolling against me, rubbing, laughing until pleasure would take us, pulling us into its own rising currents, making us move in jerky, syncopated movements, clutching and breathing hard.

Springtime came that way too, bursting up with bright bobbing blossoms, then sweeping through in unusually warm days scented with heather, narcissus, plum, cherry, apple, and peach. Your hands would sweep over my body, into my body, brushing the hairs, holding my shoulders tight. Your lips would open my lips and your tongue would take me teasingly, gently, then with greater and greater insistence. "Now," I would cry and you would

11

speed up just that fraction and hold the rhythm you knew would carry me up and out into bright explosions of color and sound.

Springtime markets were filled with fresh produce: kale and asparagus and those first incredible strawberries. I fed you the strawberries one by one, your fingers planted deep inside me. We ate grapes together and loved and talked about the past, dreamed about the future, expanded the propitious present in all directions.

Your lips were parted there above me, cranberry and rubies, your lips and the faun grey hairs along your temples filled my gaze. Your fingers moved inside me and I closed my eyes following the movements, the pauses, the sigh of want, the opening and spreading of desire.

The wisteria opened and spread across the porch, clematis in a white radiance wavered above the door. Spicy madrone perfumed the evening air. Early butterflies appeared darting among magenta shooting stars, lavender trillium, and chocolate lilies speckled with yellow and brown. Manzanita dripped with blooms clustered like milky, rosy chandeliers.

Sometimes I say it's unreasonable that I'm so happy, that I work so hard and still I'm happy; tired often, yes, but joyous, celebratory. Love can do this to me, lust too. How nice to have them combined.

Combined like our bodies rubbing and blending last night, late, both of us tired yet stirred by longing, me sliding my body down yours, feeling the hair of your legs against my crotch, against my breasts, the feel of your crispy hairs against my mouth, your odor, so delicate, so distinctly yours, fruity, earthy, pine forests in the late afternoon heat.

I rub my way into you searching for your softness, for your wetness, nest my way in and stay, dreaming of the mists rising in the mornings, of trees hidden and exposed.

I lick upward, springtime rain on my face, streams moving swiftly, rivers swollen and rich with silt. I lick upward, moisture poised on every leaf and stalk, glittering on the dandelions and buttercups, on wild strawberry blooms.

I tongue you, your liquid splashing my cheeks, subtle perfumes rising, your cries in my ears. I tongue you until you cry out and heave yourself into my face and cradle my head. And then I move more slowly, gently: focusing love.

Each year with you the springtime enters differently yet each one buds and finds us open. Early greens expand through a mist of russet and rose, yellow greens and mint tones, chartreuse and emerald hues.

Each April the fiddle heads of the bracken fern push up and unfurl. Vetch and lupine open out with the dogwood, with Indian paint brush. I spread beneath you, skin on skin, mouth on mouth, I spread and rise. Spring's heart throbs in the screaming cerise of black currant blossoms, in the faultless yellow of Oregon grape. And I come, and I come, and I come.

Late in the spring the sunny days alternate with rain, the grass grows quickly, robins sing. The jays grow huge. Bachelor's buttons make a soft blue blanket along the roadways. California poppies bloom golden in the gullies. Red columbine appears with sudden intensity. Wild lilac drapes itself gracefully, dripping with pale lavender blossoms. The smells embrace me.

White daisies gather in every open space; yellow ones perch on the hillsides, cling to small openings in sharp inclines, promising next years glory in their maturing seeds.

Each year, my love, your body close, your caring touch, each year in bursting glory, I feel the fluids rise.

Tucson in September

Tucson in September is hot. A light dry breeze kisses the skin. Sometimes storm clouds mass and Dust Devils fly. A brief windy deluge will be followed by more sun-baked days, more restive mild nights.

Fruits ripen in back yards, hang over fences into sandy alleyways. Lemons turn yellow, oranges russet up, pomegranates and figs swell. Late summer grapes hang, filled with luscious invitations.

The Catalina foothills, with their stately saguaro cactus, loom across the northern horizon. Lacy mesquite shudders gracefully in the breeze. Palo verde's small yellow flowers sparkle, their interiors dotted with red tears.

Equinox comes with a waxing moon in the evening sky, with a dawn that's bright and crisp as ripening fruit.

Marilee and Lil share a lingering kiss before Lil dresses and leaves for work. Marilee, Lil's ex-lover, is hanging out in Tucson, hanging out in Lil's bed, in her arms, recovering from yet another failed relationship.

Lil is not complaining.

Marilee breakfasts on black coffee, nude, in the enclosed yard. She thinks about Pat, the woman she has just left, about Pat and the nine or ten other great loves of her life. They were all interesting, exciting, appealing women. Something always went wrong.

Lil had been the fourth great love in her life, the first after her college years, the first of her mature loves. Over the years Lil has come to be family, willing to give her a place to rest, quiet in which to gain perspective.

After a second cup of coffee, Marilee slowly oils her entire body. She knows that there is something essentially wrong with the way she's approaching life and love but the exact nature of her error still eludes her. She carefully works oil over her neck, her elbows, between and around her toes, into her dry heels.

Later, she'll figure her problems out later.

Moving to the shade of the ramada, she settles on a large rattan couch covered with a once bright Mexican blanket, the colors now muted by the brutal glare of the Arizona sun. The blanket's rough texture presses jarringly into her flesh as she clips and files her nails.

She identifies her ex-lovers by the cities in which their love flowered, fruited, went to seed: Santa Monica, Fort Lauderdale, New Orleans, Atlanta, Houston, San Francisco. Oh, yes, San Francisco, Callie in San Francisco. God what a time that was.

At thirty-eight she feels herself poised for a new awareness, a new understanding of herself. Poised and a little desperate. She doesn't want the future to be a repeat of the last twenty years, dreams embraced and then shattered, friendships formed tenuously and then annihilated as her primary relationships dissolved.

Lil, though, has been a constant. Thank god for Lil, for her understanding, her acceptance of the vagaries of Marilee's affection, of her desire.

Like ghosts, Marilee's former lovers hover, unasked for visitors disturbing the texture of her day. She lights a joint, rests her fingers between her legs tapping lightly.

☆ ☆ ☆

Lil is quite simply pleased to have Marilee's presence in the house, her company in bed, her lively body and sexual appetite. Lil remembers feeling almost consumed by Marilee's desires when they lived together. The feeling was not always unpleasant.

Lil's most recent lover left several months ago, wanting more intensity, more commitment, more willingness to struggle through the difficulties caused by differences in temperament, in age, in backgrounds, in daily rhythms.

"I am the way I am," Lil said, stacking dishes neatly in the dishwasher. "I've been this way a long time. Take it or leave it."

The woman left.

Lil likes what she calls "bed warmers." Women who don't demand a great deal of her beyond snuggling and pussy licking and hot rubbing. She likes her clothes and environment to be neat, clean and comfortable. She wants the same from most of her lovers.

Marilee is the one exception, the wild card, the storm that stirs her deeply, makes her life more vivid.

Lil bites with relish into a deviled ham on whole wheat. She finds a meditative peace in putting small worlds together. In the model railroad store where she works, she gets a high watching the trains zip along the tracks, lights blinking, puffs of smoke shooting up like soft exclamation marks. It continues to have a quality of magic for her even though she knows how every inch of it fits together. It's a magic she can dream into, a world that is orderly and controlled.

Evenings when she's alone, she drinks wine coolers and reads her way through one classic novel after another. She prefers Thomas Hardy, Dickens, Lawrence Durell. Marilee always chides her about not supporting women writers but Lil says she just can't help liking what she likes.

At lunchtime Lil sits outside the store remembering some of their antics, like the trip she and Marilee took to Canada, sleeping on a foam pad in the back of her station wagon. "Fucking our way to Canada," Marilee always called it.

Then there were the women's movement conferences that Marilee dragged her off to saying, "It's good for them to see a unreformed butch now and then. Anyway you dance better than anyone I know."

Lil remembers Texas two-stepping her way through endless evenings when other women were waving their

16

arms in the air, looking like they were trying to come on the dance floor. Lil preferred her sex in private with one or two close friends. These group orgies, dressed, pretending you weren't doing or wanting to do just exactly what you were doing and wanting to do. Well, it just wasn't her style.

Lil finishes her sandwich and carefully smoothes the brown paper bag against her khaki covered thigh. She squints at the mountains, yellow grey against the sky.

That Marilee, though, she was always ready for sex, given any semblance of privacy at all. There were coat closets and back rooms and roadside rest stops that still set Lil's heart to racing.

She's quite a woman, that Marilee.

☆ ☆ ☆

Marilee rouses.

She remembers that she should be editing her next book. She doesn't know why, even when her personal life is in shambles, she can still write coherently about goals and strategies, can move women to action by her words. Lil calls it a gift. Marilee feels like two very different people, one confident and outgoing, the other confused, muddling along, wondering where she went wrong, what to do next.

A vision of Pat, angry, in Albuquerque two weeks ago, comes to her mind. When Pat learned about the casual "conference affair" she was having with a women's studies teacher from a neighboring state, the shit had really hit the fan, as Lil would say.

Marilee goes into the kitchen to fix something to eat. Pat had certainly been damned angry for someone who had thought she wanted an open relationship. The scene had been filled with accusations and dishes smashed. Some neighbor had called the police. Pat had gone off to get drunk and Marilee had been gone by the time she got back.

Marilee is good at packing and leaving quickly.

She puts leftover tamale pie in the microwave and slices cucumbers. One of the nice things about coming back to Lil's is knowing where everything is, knowing her way around, knowing what to expect. She finishes off the unsmoked half of an earlier joint while setting out the food, getting a cold Diet Pepsi from the fridge.

She thinks she's smoking more than she should but is reluctant to cut back when she's in transition. She especially likes to smoke before meals and before sex. It seems to improve her focus, make the sensations so much stronger. Perhaps the dope is part of her problem with relationships, but the connection is tenuous compared to the pleasure it brings into her life.

While eating, she reads a porn book about three beauties snowed into a cabin on a mountaintop, getting it on with strap-on dildos. The feminist in her is appalled by the text but her cunt obviously likes it, causing her to reach again between her legs. In the story, two of the women are using the dildos to enter the third both vaginally and anally. The third woman is driven into a frenzy of lust by their repeated, rhythmic thrustings. All three of the women orgasm simultaneously, "Ah, ah, ah, oh, ah!" Marilee comes soon after, straddling the kitchen chair, clutching the book to her breast, oblivious.

She rests before finishing lunch and restoring the kitchen to order. She seems to be resting a lot lately, wonders where her energy has gone.

She goes outside to swim, the heat hitting her like a wall, the water a primal bath. She does slow laps thinking about her parents, how they would disapprove of the way she's living her life, spending the money they left in trust for her. That small but steady independent income has financed her movement work as well as funding her escape from relationships in crisis.

Perhaps if she had not been able to afford to leave, she might have stayed to form a more lasting bond with someone. Maybe yes, maybe no.

18

Money had certainly kept her mother tied to her father's side.

She dries and stretches again in the shade of the ramada, darker now that the sun is on the other side of the house. She dreams of an elegant woman coming out of water, striding across hot shimmery sands to envelop her in her arms, kissing passionately. She dreams herself pushed back into cool satiny sheets, pushed back and down, taken forcefully yet with great delicacy by a woman who seems to be both outside and inside her body, privy to her inner person.

The woman drags her body over Marilee's body, rubbing skin to skin, bone to bone, then slowly straddles her face and lets her kiss her into orgasm in a most gratifying manner.

Their dream bodies are slick with their fruitings. Mangoes and avocados drop from the trees around them.

"Stay where you are," the woman tells her. "Stay where you are loved."

She wakes slowly, carrying the dream with her. In a mood of detachment she showers, dresses in a loose shift, and wanders through the house touching the familiar details of Lil's life.

In the kitchen she removes tacos from the fridge, grates cheese, puts refried beans into a pan, but doesn't start them heating.

She decides not to smoke another joint.

Lil comes in with roses and wine.

"Hi, sweetie. How's my favorite girl?" Lil kisses her playfully then gives the kiss more and more of her attention. "Mum, so I shouldn't leave you alone all day, is that it?"

"I'm just very glad to see you home." She gives Lil a squeeze, turns and heats the beans.

Facing each other across the dinner table Lil offers a toast. "To us," she says, eyes merry. "To us and all our future and former lovers. May they never meet and compare notes."

The Storm Raged

The storm raged. It had been blowing and raining for days. Sometimes sleet fell, sometimes small bright hail stones. The roads were not safe, but the cabin was cozy, warmed by a wood fire, lit by candles and by kerosene lamps.

They made love, endlessly, touching each other in private places, hidden sacred places, finding new positions, delicate shadings of old feelings, repeating nuances of delight.

The one kept smelling her fingers, sweet body secretions, inhaling stimulants so intense she felt transported. She'd lie beside the other, listening to her read, one hand tucked near her face, two fingers of the other buried gently in her lover.

Now and then she'd move her fingers until the other's voice would break.

"Cunt, cunt, cunt," she'd sing, soft and low. "Pussy, pussy, pussy. I love my lover's pussy."

"Silly," the other would say, smiling. Her smile dissolved as clinchings took her body, as the expanse of pleasure muscle responded.

The one would stop then, would wait. The other would roll her head languorously, sigh, and resume reading.

Or, the other would lay the book flat on her chest and push into the one's fingers, humping them, rotating against them. "Please, please," she'd say. "Please darling, I love you. Please make me come."

And the other would.

The storm raged on, throwing sheets of rain against the windows, tossing branches which would thump against the roof. The long extended twilight would dissolve into immense, magnificent, enshrouding night.

Sometimes when the one was cooking on the wood stove the other would call out, "Sweet love, come sit on my face." The one would move the pot to the back of the stove and come and come, bay leaves and thyme filling the air, basil and tarragon, garlic and root smells, oregano and marjoram, curry and ginger.

At times the one would dress for the other, dress in silky, slinky clothes, scarves, shawls; dress to be felt, to be admired, to have her clothing reached under, her nipples excited through the veil of cloth.

The other would watch her dress, or perhaps would be asleep and wake to find the one rubbing against her, trailing slippery cloth across receptive skin.

The other always responded.

During lulls in the storm they would dress warmly and bring in wood from the shed, noting the accumulated drifts of damp leaves, the pine needles matting the ground. Wood smoke, ozone, and evergreen scented the air.

Inside again, the other would perfume herself with a mint or spice, an exotic talc or essence from some wild shore. The one would inhale deeply, press against her or crouch above her weaving a pattern around her with her nose and then her tongue.

"You taste so sweet," she'd say when she got down to the other's fur. And then she'd bury her face against those bearded nether lips and lick and suck, lick and suck.

"I want more of you," the other would say and slowly the one would move around until her legs straddled the other's face, her cunt dipping to the other's mouth, the other's fingers playing with her openings.

"We've been in bed for days," the one said, showing no inclination to move.

"True, true, but look at all the exercise we've gotten."

Yet, shortly they rose and began dancing, moving to the sound of the windcalls, to the rhythm of the rain splashing against glass, against the metal of the roof. They moved slowly at first then with greater extensions until they reached a frenzied climax of shimmied contact.

Falling back into bed, their bodies danced against each other again in the rolling, sliding motions of thighs and buttocks, breasts and hands.

Later the one sat filing her nails, painting them a fiery tone while the other read. When the polish dried the one began to massage the other using oil which she warmed in her hands before sliding it onto the other's skin. The oil was fragrant, fruity, amber colored, luxuriant. The one closed her eyes as she worked, melting into the other's flesh, pressing against and along the muscles, praising the bones beneath. Time moved as slowly as her hands, imprinting love.

She slid down, breathing on her lover, on her beloved's body, exhaling warmth, caring, lust.

"Here, come here, come here for me," she crooned, stroking and rubbing. "Here, here, follow me here, notice what I'm doing, come for me now."

And her lover came, not quickly but with gratifying quivers and many sounds.

Stirring later, the other said, "I almost came just thinking about the color of your nails."

"I'll have to do it again, soon," the one answered.

"I'm sure you will," the other replied, reaching for her, smiling.

Ginny's Defense

The phone rang late, about half-past nine. I was reading. Ginny should be home from class soon.

"R-Rena, something's happened." Ginny was crying. "C-Could you come get me? I'm scared." She's hiccuping and crying and something else. What could have happened? There'd been no trouble around the University in a long time.

"Where are you? Do you need an ambulance? Are you OK until I get there?"

"I'm in my office with the door locked. Someone — look, I'm not hurt, I'm all right, just shaken. Please hurry."

"Yeah, yeah, fifteen minutes."

I've known Ginny a long time. Hell, we've been together for five years. Things don't shake her easily. I grabbed my jacket, a blanket for her since the night had turned cool, and hurried to the van, "The Belle of Homeyness."

"Come on Belle, lets see what's happening." I keyed the ignition and she came alive like the reliable angel she is. We nosed out, downhill to the main drag, me cursing stoplights and slow moving cars.

I hope it's nothing sexual. Things have been going so well lately with Ginny talking to a counselor about what happened in her past, her dad touching her at night and all.

Sometimes, now, she'll start making love to me, or tell me she wants sex. That never used to happen. It feels

23

more balanced this way, not me always wanting and her turning away often as not, saying, "I just can't. It's like a blank wall inside me. I run up against it and there's no way around."

I didn't really mind a whole lot. There were so many other things we did together: softball and camping and a bit of mountain climbing. Still, I'd always wished that sex was easier, less iffy, smoother, like the way we canoed or set up camp or built fires.

We were out camping the first time she told me about her dad. It was one of those dark, starless, windy nights. We were sitting around the fire.

"He was real loving, not mean to me at all," she said. "Mother didn't like sex. She often said so. Sometime when I was eleven or twelve," she pauses to put a branch on the fire, "he started coming into my room, late. He'd sit down next to me and stroke me through the covers, talking the whole time. He told me about what it was like when he was a kid and the things he did with his cousins on the farm and how he loved me and didn't want to hurt me. It must have been summer, the bed covers were light."

She clutched her mug of hot chocolate, forgetting to drink. I kept one arm loosely around her, wanting her to feel loved and protected but free at the same time.

"He'd put his hand under the cover and touch me between my legs and something wonderful and scary would happen to my body and then he'd stop and kiss me and go away."

I put more wood on the fire as she continued talking.

"I always felt sick to my stomach afterward. He was my dad and I loved him but I didn't want him doing that to me. Yet I never told him to stop." She blew her nose hard and wiped her eyes.

"If he hadn't died so suddenly when I was fifteen I don't know what would have happened, how it would have ended. I always felt it was God punishing us for what we'd been doing. I was sure I was to blame. And then my uncle raped me, a few weeks after the funeral. I just went to pieces, wouldn't go to school, cried all the time. They thought it was grief about my dad and left me alone."

She hugged her knees, staring into the fire, still holding the mug. "I finished high school by correspondence, then went off to college on a scholarship. My mom died shortly after that and I never went back. I built a wall around what happened. I'd feel sick just thinking about it so I stopped thinking about it. I feel sick right now."

"Sometimes when we're making love I get that same sick feeling, like I'm going to throw up. Then I just can't go on. When you hold me and talk to me, it goes away. Just the sound of your voice is so comforting, so different from his."

"Is that why you like me to read you to sleep?"

"No, my grandma did that. She lived with us when I was young. My father's mother. I loved her so. She died too." Ginny poured the cold chocolate drink from the mug, wiping her cheeks with the back of her hand.

I brushed away her tears, kissed them away, then we climbed into our sleeping bags and held hands all night long. We still hold hands a lot at night.

We didn't talk much about her past, but it was always there in my memory. She would say "Stop!" and look sick and hurt and sometimes scared and I would hold her until it went away.

The steering wheel felt clammy as I turned into the parking lot behind the liberal arts building. I could see her standing in the lighted office window. Her light was out before I even had the motor off and then she was running from the back door, books and purse clutched against her.

I met her halfway and put my arm around her even though we didn't usually do that on campus. She was laughing and crying at the same time. She hurried me to the van.

"Belle and Rena to the rescue," she said, putting her

25

books in the back, wrapping the blanket around her and moving in close.

"Somebody, a guy, grabbed me when I started to the bus, after class. He had a knife and said he would kill me if I screamed. 'Stick' me was the word he used. He pushed me up against the wall and shoved his hand inside my clothes, into my pants.

"At first I just didn't believe it was happening, then I felt sick, then I got sick, literally. My dinner came up all over him and me too, spaghetti and the remains of meatballs and spinach. What a mess." She wiped her eyes and looked at me, half-grinning.

"He let go of me and started yelling that I'd ruined his outfit and he had to go to work later. Then he gave me a shove and ran off. I went back in and called you and cleaned up. It's so hard to sort out my reactions. I've been shaking ever since, but I feel elated."

"What about the police? Are you up to talking with them?"

"Mummm, I want them to know he's around. I just couldn't face them alone."

"Want to call or go over to security or down to the station?"

"Let's call from my office. We'd probably have to come back here anyway."

She called both the town cops and the campus police who kept calling her "Dr. Burton" and had her walk through the scene pointing out where the creep grabbed her and where she threw up.

"That was quite a defense, Dr. Burton, quite a defense," the lieutenant kept repeating, shaking his head.

They never found out who did it.

Ginny dreamed about the attack and her response for weeks, waking me in the middle of the night for comfort, apologizing and shaking. In each dream the amount she vomited became greater. Sometimes the villain became her uncle, later still her father. One night she said it was like a river coming out of her, a flood with houses and trees and cars being washed away. After that the dreams ceased.

We didn't make love for a long time after the attack. She got into a support group for incest survivors which seemed to help a lot. When we did start making love it was like starting to get to know each other all over again. We went very slow, with a lot of long pauses and a number of full stops, sometimes for months at a time. What was different was a peacefulness about how we were together, a sense of comfort.

One night she turned to me and said, "The wall is gone. I don't understand where or how. I still think of the past at times but if I start feeling sick I remember the river, the feeling of everything flowing out of me, and the feeling goes away." That was the first night that sex felt really graceful between us, graceful and natural. We moved easily together.

There are still rough times, times she turns away, but they come seldom and pass quickly. And it's all been worth it, the waiting and the struggle to understand. I wouldn't trade my Ginny for anyone in the world. Even when the nightmares come I know that good times will follow. That's part of hanging in there, part of working things out.

Touched By Light

Lisamarie stands in a shaft of sunlight, in an old-fashioned, elegant room, facing a freestanding mirror. She's dressed in a yellow print that pulses with the light. She spreads her bare feet against the polished wood as she watches her hands press against her dress, against her body. The damp smell of the stone walls contrasts with her own heat rising. Her eyes are half closed, her cheeks flushed.

Earlier she had returned from lunch in the piazza, pausing to watch her favorite fountain, baroque figures writhing, water spurting like rockets. Peace had been hers.

Entering the pensione she'd been greeted by the owner's son. "Signorina Talie, wait! A letter!"

"Grazie, Frederico." Taking the long envelop she smiled at the handsome youth. "How are your English lessons coming."

"Quite fine, Miss Talie." Frederico smiled back as he repeatedly tossed and caught a heavy set of keys.

"Addio," she said, glancing at the letter as she walked toward the stairs.

She stopped and looked again, wanting to discount the reality of the embossed words:
FROM THE LAW OFFICES OF SARAH R. LEWIS AND ASSOCIATES.

Panic gripped her and she hurried for the privacy of her third floor room, taking the stairs two at a time. She

28

locked the door behind her and leaned against it, panting, the acrid smell of fear rising about her.

She had fled from Sarah and that impossible triangle, fled San Francisco, old friends, comfortable habits. Settling in Rome, she'd consoled herself that Sarah was half a world away. Sarah who had wanted everything: a wife, a mistress and a fancy career. Lisamarie had been the mistress.

As she crosses to the bed, Lisamarie glimpses the wild beauty of her disarray, her bright, dark eyes and unruly hair. She tosses the letter onto a pillow, sits and removes her shoes. Rising, she steps into the light, before the mirror and examines herself, first with her eyes, then with her hands.

"Here I am," she thinks, "thirty-five years old, a literary translator, a single woman, a lover of women." Not just "women" though, at least not since she'd met Sarah four years before. Sarah had filled her vision, captured her emotions, beckoned her on, yet always withheld commitment.

"I've been with Kate for twelve years," Sarah told Lisamarie. "She believed in me through all the rough times. I wouldn't leave her now."

Lisamarie admired Sarah's loyalty. If anything it made her more attractive. Lisamarie couldn't explain or justify her obsession with Sarah. It had simply existed, full-blown, from the moment they met. It had ruled her life.

Walking to the sideboard, she pours water and drinks it, then splashes a little on her face.

"Why now?" she asks the empty air. "Why is she writing me now?" Lisamarie begins to pace. As she moves she stretches, fluidly passing into the old warm-up routine that had once been a daily regime, now remembered more by her body than by her waking mind. She flexes each set of muscles in turn, manipulates and rotates her joints. As she moves, images of Sarah float before her.

29

She'd been hired to translate legal papers. Her first meeting with Sarah left her with a vivid impression: a voluptuous powerhouse of a woman whose heavy, straight hair swung like dark wings against her cheeks, soft eyes behind perfectly round, thin-rimmed glasses. Perfectly matched dimples appeared on each cheek, seeming to have a life of their own.

When Lisamarie turned in the completed project, she had stared at Sarah's hands with their short-cropped nails, the sapphire on her little finger. The smell of fresh cut roses filled the room.

"Have lunch with me," Sarah said, tilting her head back, light refracting off her glasses, dimples playing near the corners of her mouth.

They ate in a glass covered patio, intimate, expensive. Banana trees, bamboo, and traveler's palm encircled them, filtering the light. Napkins and tablecloths were springtime green. The color seemed to vibrate and echo inside her, promising growth somehow, expansion, a luxury of possibilities.

Lisamarie wondered if her excitement was visible.

The waitress obviously knew Sarah well, arriving with a lemonade before any order had been placed.

"Everything's good here. Indulge yourself," Sarah said, flashing a smile with the dimples this time.

Lisamarie ordered the first item on the menu, the first drink on the list. Her eyes returned to Sarah who seemed to be studying her.

The waitress disappeared. White doves called to each other from a floor-to-ceiling cage. The air seemed extraordinarily bright, crystalline.

"Are you involved with anyone?" Sarah asked, lifting one eyebrow.

"No," Lisamarie smoothed the tablecloth, took a drink, wondered how far Sarah would go with her questioning.

"You are a lesbian, though, aren't you?"

Lisamarie choked on her water. The room felt very hot, the food smells overbearing. She forced herself to meet Sarah's gaze. "Yes. Yes, I am." Breathe deeply. Go for Alpha. Wait.

"Good. I find you very attractive. Would you be interested in an affair, no strings attached?" Sarah removed her glasses, continued to gaze into Lisamarie's eyes.

There it was, the offer of a fantasy situation that had drifted through Lisamarie's dreams for years. Sensations that moments before had only rippled, were now a roar beneath her skin. Lisamarie started to shake.

Sarah reached across the table, covering her hand. "I'm sorry. I didn't mean to upset you."

Lisamarie felt the physical contact like an electric current, felt her skin go warm, her sex parts throb, a dampness on her face, between her legs. Inexplicably, she felt very young and, as when she was young, she wanted to cry over receiving exactly the kind of attention she had been wanting.

"It's all right. I'm all right." Lisamarie inhaled, sorting excitement from panic. "And yes, I am interested."

Lisamarie pauses in her calisthenic movements, draws closer to the mirror, notices how the light seems to wrap around her, caressing her. The sunshine here has a bright whiteness to it, a luminescence similar to that other city of her love, of her and Sarah's love. Is that part of the attraction here, part of the excitement, the comfort?

She unfastens and pulls her dress over her head, then smooths the gloss of her cream-colored slip which seems, in this light, lit from within. Her nipples, erect, push out firmly. Sarah always started there, with her breasts. She would touch them lingeringly, lovingly, kneading and rolling them in her strong hands, breathing on them through the cloth of whatever garment Lisamarie was wearing. She would rub her face and cheek against them when they were, rarely, bare.

31

Sarah had a way of concentrating on her breasts that could almost make Lisamarie come without any other form of stimulation. Her touching would go on and on, Lisamarie arching and moaning, pushing herself against Sarah, against her hand and leg, squeezing her thighs in anticipation, acknowledging her lust.

They had made love on the heavily carpeted office floor, on the leather covered couch with its soft touch, its rich smell. Whenever Lisamarie was with Sarah, she felt cherished. Sometimes in the evenings flowers would arrive, exotic blossoms filling up her rooms with their brilliance and seductive odors.

Sarah brought her gifts: Lapis blue earrings flecked with gold, a malachite box whose green whorls soothed her eyes, a mother of pearl comb, inlaid bracelets, a jade ring.

Lisamarie continued with her translating work even though Sarah offered to support her. She did not tell her friends about the affair, or mention it to her family. Always she watched for a glimpse of Sarah, listened for the ringing of the phone.

From outside the fabric of the slip, Lisamarie touches her breasts in the warm light, watching her hands move in slow motion, like watching someone else's hands. She wonders again about the letter, decides to put it from her mind for a while longer.

Slowly she removes the slip, watching. Making a pad out of a towel she carefully stands on her head, enjoying her legs unfolding upward. Closing her eyes she feels the weight, the varying tensions. Pointing her toes she stretches as far as possible, holding the position until her legs begin to tremble. She opens her eyes and follows her legs down.

"Not bad for someone as out of shape as I am," she thinks, watching the play of light flowing around and over her. As her first leg touches the floor, she sees her vulva flair, notices how the hairs seem to spring away from it like little exclamation points. Giggles, like champagne bubbles, are beginning to rise inside her.

She studies her breasts, a ripe handful as Sarah used to say. She would chuckle as she reached beneath a jacket or under a sweater, sigh as she slid her hand behind a neckline or beneath a blouse.

Her favorite form of sex though, was to watch Lisamarie touch herself, seated in the fine old Queen Anne chair with its velvety wings, one leg hung over the arm rest, a towel under her in case the fluids ran.

It wasn't that Sarah only wanted to watch. Sometimes she would make love to Lisamarie across the broad mahogany desk, or leaning against the wooden file cabinet that had belonged to her grandfather, the one who'd raised her.

But most often, in their second and third year together, Sarah would want Lisamarie to touch herself, half sprawled on the rose-colored chair, her skirt raised, her shoes still on, a frond from the potted palm draped over her shoulder.

"You are so beautiful," she would say, kneeling before Lisamarie.

Lisamarie would lick her fingers and reach down to find herself moist already, excited by the cross-town trip, the whole fantasy-like adventure of entering this venerable office, masturbating and, finally, coming for the pleasure it gave them both.

Extending her arms, Lisamarie watches the light enfold her, revealing, exposing her to herself. Dancing particles of dust glitter against the dark backdrop of the room.

She thinks about the letter behind her, decides that, whatever it says, she doesn't have to answer.

She had written Sarah a letter when she'd first left, and a longer one when she'd settled here, secure in her room and her job. "You don't have to respond," she had said, "But I want you to know where I am and that I love you still."

For months she had gone to bed resolute but lonely and awakened crying from dreams that found her isolated in a barren landscape, running.

Slowly she'd made friends among the expatriates and the writers with whose words she spent her days. The friendships had taken hold and, although no lovers were among them, Lisamarie had welcomed the companionable hours, the intellectual stimulation.

She forces herself to remember why she'd left. What had transpired had been so simple, so slight. She'd met Sarah's long time lover and housemate, Kate.

Kate was a food columnist for a San Francisco paper, an editor of cookbooks, a passionate gardener.

"Kate wants to meet you," Sarah had said. "Can you come to dinner Wednesday?"

Lisamarie hadn't wanted to meet this woman who held Sarah so tightly bound to her. "Why?" she asked. "What does she want with me?"

"She says you're part of our life. She wants to get to know you."

Lisamarie puts on her crimson robe and begins to pace again, back and forth, crossing and recrossing the light. Running her fingers through her hair, she glances at the high window through which the light is coming, at the bleached blue sky beyond. Turning, she pulls the robe tighter, remembering.

She had obsessed about the meeting, dressed with care and arrived slightly late and out of breath. She had known the visit was a mistake as soon as Kate opened the door, smiled warmly, and extended her hand.

The first surprise had been how much older Kate was than Sarah: Kate with her casually neat gray hair, her gentle comments about what her body could no longer do.

The evening had unfolded with surprises. The house was comfortable rather than elegant, the food simple. Chopin played in the background. Kate entertained her with stories of her roses, with the antics of her five cats.

Lisamarie had understood instantly that Kate was not going to fight her, was, rather, going to accept and incorporate her into their extended family. Lisamarie felt her dreams of a life with Sarah, a life alone with Sarah, splinter and crash around her. She hadn't realized how much she'd invested in that dream until it was gone.

The light has moved closer to the mirror and Lisamarie pulls her armchair into its rectangle. Its color has warmed as the afternoon progressed. Supported within the frame of its bright definition, she leans toward the mirror and says, "I Love You," to her reflection before sitting in the chair, unfastening her robe and settling her leg high over its softly padded arm.

She begins to touch herself, that old pleasure she has forgone in Sarah's absence.

She touches herself and watches as her fingers stroke her long curves, caressed by the sunlight as well as her own flesh. The sound of distant traffic fades completely as she smells her fingers, delicately touches them to her tongue, slowly sucks them before lowering them again.

Her mind touches on her loving Sarah, on her respect for Kate. With a new sureness about what she has done, about what she is doing, she realizes a new love and respect for herself. Without regretting the past, she has moved on.

She touches herself with a practiced economy of motion, a streamlined pleasure bringing joy in ever increasing waves. Turning inward, she's left with areolas of light, a warm glow pulses against her lids.

She merges with the light in a fluid extension of feeling, merges and submerges and finally sleeps. She dreams of flowers blossoming all around her. Flowers, larger than she is, sway on hairy stems. Poppies, graceful and floppy, unfold, petal by petal. A hot rainbow of poppies embraces her, shelters her.

When she wakes the light is gone. She moves stiffly, her sluggish mind searching, circling in until she finds

35

the letter, first in memory, then where she'd left it on the bed.

Lisamarie turns on the bedside lamp, fluffs the pillows and climbs under the covers. She sniffs the letter, nothing, then opens it and reads:

Beloved, I have hoped you would come back. I love you still. Nothing's changed. I can't leave Kate. Surely you understand.

Won't you return? I ache to see you and hold you in my arms.

Lisamarie smiles. How like Sarah to want everything her way, on her terms.

Taking out her stationary she writes:

I'm happy here, Sarah, I won't be coming back. I remember you with fondness and wish you well. My love to you both.

The Flowered Screen

In the sixties Amy lived as part of a polysexual communal family whose primary income was from stained glass work and marijuana. Their home base was in northern California from which they traveled to craft fairs selling cleverly wrought boxes, mirrors, lamps, and windows. In the evenings pot would be dispensed along with the folk songs and comradery.

Amy loved selling crafts, interacting with people, finding just the right item to put in someone's hands or call to their attention.

Her lovers were both men and women, sometimes individually, sometimes in groups.

In the early seventies she had a son, Rob, and her life shifted. The commune broke up, individuals and pairs scattered along the coast and inland. Some went (or returned) to the East. Amy moved with Rob to San Francisco, got work in a crafts shop. After managing the shop for some years she started a gallery of her own featuring stained glass and exquisite handmade jewelry. She thrived.

She favored women lovers but never brought them home until Denise, her son's third grade teacher, won Rob's heart and then her own.

Years passed with joy and ease. They bought a house, vacationed in the woods, subscribed to the ballet.

No matter what the weather, the sun seemed to shine upon them. Amy never thought about it ending.

Denise died. Quietly, at work, her heart stopped.

There had been no warning.

"Sometimes it just happens that way, a birth defect that goes unnoticed, an anomaly. No one could have predicted it. Nothing could have been done. We're sorry."

Rob and Amy grieved together. Amy thought her pain would never end.

She worked diligently but without passion, thankful to have something to occupy her mind. Evenings she sat before her gas log fire thinking of suicide. Her love of Rob and his for her kept her alive.

In the spring of the second year Amy took up gardening as a distraction, found she loved tending plants in all kinds of weather. She nurtured their fledgling growth, enjoyed their maturity. She favored plants with dark, shiny foliage, with elaborately shaped flowers.

Rob went away to college, graduated, went into the service.

A decade after Denise's death, Megan, twelve years her junior, entered Amy's life through the gallery, bringing photographs of her stained glass windows and a list of satisfied clients.

"I need someone to help me with the business side of art," she said.

It felt like the sun was peeping through. Amy was very interested in Megan.

Amy visited her studio, was enchanted by the work, primarily floral, throbbingly colored. Work in progress covered the tables of the large, light-filled room. Completed projects lined the massive windows.

Amy felt her physical self disappear into the hues and tones, the subtleties of shape and shading. She experienced the glass in a very visceral way. A very sexual way. It was a bit disconcerting but not at all unpleasant.

38

Megan invited her up into the living loft for tea. The space was all dark wood, cedar smells, soft chairs, and an unobtrusive double bed. Persian rugs covered the floor. A small efficient kitchen nestled into one wall.

Megan pulled out art books, talked quietly and intensely about what she was trying to do, what she hoped to accomplish both with the glass and with her career. "I want to make people really notice glass as an art form." She spread photographs and drawings across the table and rug, her voice warm with excitement. "I want my panels and windows to be exhibited in museums."

Her words formed effervescent pictures in Amy's mind.

Amy became her dealer.

They met once or twice a week throughout the autumn and winter, looking at slides and pictures, visiting galleries and exhibitions. Amy felt a deep pleasure whenever they were together, a thrill whenever Megan looked at or touched her. Megan remained a little removed, her feeling opaque to Amy's inquiring glance.

In the early spring, Amy invited Megan to her home for dinner. In preparation she installed new lights in the garden and a heater in the enclosed patio. She pretended to herself that she wasn't overly excited, teased herself for feeling like a school girl.

Megan loved the house and garden, noticed all the fine details, the thoughtful juxtapositions of sculpture and paintings, the flowers beautifully arranged.

Dinner lasted late into the night. They lingered over brandy, talking and laughing. Megan kissed her lightly on the forehead before leaving. "Thank you, thank you, Amy, you're wonderful to be with. You're wonderful to me."

Amy leaned against the door long after she had gone.

On Sundays throughout the spring, Megan came to draw the flowers and leaves in Amy's walled garden. Later they'd have Chinese food or pizza delivered and sit in the living room studying the drawings.

"You are so good, my dear," she'd say, wanting to say more, holding herself back, waiting for a sign.

From the drawings Megan produced a glass screen in three panels that held the enclosed, focused beauty of the garden.

"I want to buy it," Amy said as soon as she saw it.

"Let me give it to you."

"No."

"Why not?"

"Because I covet it. I want to *own* it."

Megan acquiesced with grace.

In August, Megan asked Amy to go to a dance with her. Amy agreed, suggesting that because she had a car, she could pick Megan up and drive them to the event being held across the bridge in Sausalito.

They had known each other exactly one year.

Amy fussed over her clothes, settling finally on something soft and flowing, apricot with deep rose accents.

Megan opened the studio door wearing silvery, punky evening clothes, sparkling gems in her ears. They stood just inside the door, looking at each other. Amy felt bathed in light.

"Here, this is for you," Megan said, taking a small box from her pocket.

Amy untied the purple ribbon, unwrapped the foil. Inside was a ring, a topaz, her birthstone. The setting was exquisite, modern without being heavy. Megan slipped it on her finger.

"I love you," Megan said. "I want to give you more."

"Yes," Amy answered. "Please."

They kissed for a very long time.

A Nourishing Affair

Julianna always liked the feel of something inside her. As a teenager she liked candles: white ones for purity, red for excitement, purple for queer. She still prefers candles when traveling.

Some years ago she started experimenting with vegetables: zucchini, cucumber, dakon radish. Currently she favors carrots.

Grocery shopping has become a delight. Anticipation builds as she lingers near the cunty cheeses, fingering the blue, the brie, the roquefort, the camembert. She chants their names quietly, remembered tastes exploding in her mind.

Usually she chooses a cheese to take home with her for a snack. Sometimes, though, she takes several, feeling greedy, deliciously greedy. Today she takes one of each.

Slowing for the pastas she remembers her grandmother's dinners redolent with garlic, with freshly grated parmesan, romano, with mozzarella, with the comforting aroma of olive oil. She slips a few packages of linguini into her cart, promising herself a pesto sauce soon or a creamy clam sauce later.

She approaches the fresh foods section last, excitement leaping in her veins. Rounding the corner from condiments she pauses to admire the long rows of glistening produce, artfully piled.

She gathers kiwi, oranges, bananas, sniffing her way down the row. Moving on, she admires the kale with its suggestive convolutions, chard, spinach with its deep coloration, the decorative lines of the beet greens, the floppy delicacy of the mustard.

Deeply, she inhales.

Approaching the root vegetables, her pulse begins to race: turnips, rutabagas, parsnips, carrots. Ah, carrots.

She passes over the ones in bags, taking her time to examine the loose piled bodies, choosing for size, for curve, for smoothness, for certain desirable bumps.

Sometimes she becomes sure that her secret prurient interest shows, that her radiant expectancy must broadcast to everyone in the area.

No one seems to notice.

She bags her choices and hurries her cart to the front of the market, suddenly impatient. A rush of eager buoyancy warms her as she waits in the check-out line.

No one notices at all, yet she feels utterly self-conscious, totally exposed.

Check out finally completed, she walks uphill quickly, savoring thoughts of one carrot, warmed in hot water, trimmed, ready.

Pigeons scatter before her. The sun, which earlier had been out, is now hidden behind a layer of clouds.

She reaches her building and hurries up the steps. The building manager turns from his mailbox to hold the door for her.

"Ah, yes, Miss Nicholson, I'm glad to see you just now. The plumber is here today. He'll check your apartment soon. Just needs to finish downstairs."

"Right." Damn and double damn. The waiting, though, can have a salutary effect. Julianna holds the carrot clearly in her mind.

She unpacks, shelves, and refrigerates her purchases, distantly aware of movements in the building, of comings and goings and bangings. The carrots sit on the counter.

She smiles whenever she glimpses them. Soon, she promises herself, soon.

The plumber arrives, replaces all her washers, checks for other leaks, cleans the catch in her bathroom sink.

She sees him indistinctly, her skin feeling peppery, her breathing shallow.

"That's it, lady. You're all fixed up."

She thanks him, closes and double locks the door and leans against it, collecting her energies, focusing.

She goes to the bathroom, turns on the wall heater and starts running a bath, filling the water with bath beads, lighting candles.

Returning to the kitchen, she spreads the carrots out, makes her final selection and refrigerates the rest. She washes and trims and dries her special friend and carries it into the bedroom, placing it precisely where she will want to find it later.

She returns to the bathroom, strips, examines her body with pleasure in the long mirror. She steps jauntily in, whistling the theme from "The Way We Were."

She considers her two years of celibacy, the clarity and order that they have brought to her life. Before that, there was Fern. Their sex life had been great, but the wear and tear on her emotions had been excruciating.

Now she is taking time off from the intensity and conflict, time to heal, time to get to know herself better. She has learned she likes to go to movies even when there's no one around to go with her, that cooking appealing meals for herself is a pleasure. She's learned, in short, to get her eyes and mind off of others and back on herself. It's a lesson she never learned at home where everything seemed to be everyone else's business.

Finishing the bath, she parts the bubbles and rises from the foam, her own Venus reflected imprecisely back to her from the fogged glass.

She dries herself and anoints her whole body with oil, then turns off the heater, takes a fresh towel to the bedroom where she spreads it, spreads herself on it, and

43

puffs up the pillows under her head. She lets the remnants of her nighttime typesetting job, her daily personality, slip away. This time alone, more than any other, is hers. In this most private of activities, which she has never shared with anyone, she is fully available to herself, known to herself, revealed.

With both hands she touches herself between her legs until the moisture inside flows. Her touch is firm, circular, concentrating on the glans, the mons, the fatty outer lips. She focuses her attention on sensations which spread in hot waves. Phosphorescent lights appear in spots behind her closed eyelids.

When the wetness is adequate, when her excitement is high enough, she turns onto her stomach, kneels, and inserts the carrot.

Slowly she slides her body down against the furry towel.

She presses her fingers into the spreading fire of her mons and drops her awareness to her vagina, to the fullness there, squeezing, squeezing against that fullness, pulling the energy, the tightness inside her, inhaling and inhaling again, deeply. It feels so good.

As her passion builds she feels herself rocking, pressing against her fingers, holding her breath. Tension pulls her body toward its center, pulls her knees against the bed. Her shoulders crab forward, pushing her face against the pillow, pulling her head and neck together, tighter, tighter into that elastic, rubbery balance, that finely tuned, quivering edge.

She loses all awareness of the room around her. Her past and future vanish. The present compresses into a crystalline gem of existence.

She rocks back and forth, concentrating on the sensations, hanging on to the edge of control, the edge of delirium. Her body takes on a life of its own, her fingers fluttering against the mounting glow centered beneath them. She tightens her thighs and buttocks, squeezes against the vaginal fullness. Her breath is harsh in her ears.

44

At that point, where intensity verges on pain, where her straining body shakes and begs for release, finally she is carried up and out of awareness, into a riot of intense, ecstatic sensations.

The pleasure suffuses her whole body, rippling, rolling outward in waves from that hot, glittery focus in her groin.

Julianna does not move for a long, long time.

When she does, she slowly turns, rubbing her hands gently over her breasts and belly, lovingly touching her thighs.

She removes the carrot and leaves it on the towel beside her. Dizzy with remembered pleasure, she moves with care around the room, putting on a soft, old velour robe and furry slippers.

She takes the carrot with her to the kitchen where she washes and slices it, then sets it aside as she prepares the rest of her dinner.

Afterglow

Maureen drove north and west, into the mountains and the setting sun. The mountains were purple and orange. The sun sprayed gilded streamers from behind bunched ropes of clouds. The sky was aqua. The radio played easy listening golden oldies, the once radical music of her college days, some twenty years before.

The hot twilight smells reminded her of those youthful years as well, reminded her of her first woman lover, courting after dinner, long slow walks between the dorm and the library, kisses stolen in an enclosed courtyard, the single bed in her small room.

Maureen was feeling intensely sexual.

The sun dropped below the mountain peaks, turning the clouds an exquisite rose, silhouetting trees along the ridge. The oncoming lights were a string of jewels along the interstate. Her breath caught at the beauty spread out before her.

She wished her lover, Winn, could be her with her, but felt the experience more vividly because of her aloneness.

Winn would be asleep by the time she reached home.

Maureen thought of Winn with her duck-tailed graying hair modified for daytime wear into a style befitting a high school principal. She smiled, remembering their lovemaking the previous night, the firm hands and pliant flesh.

46

Winn was a thoughtful, thorough lover. A dyke of the old school who had opened, over the years, to new experiences. The opening was due, at least in part, to the demands of an outgoing, aggressive lover, Nancy, from whom she was now separated.

Maureen was very grateful for the changes Nancy had made in Winn's life.

Winn had stayed open, responsive, receptive as Maureen timidly reached for her, stroking her way into Winn's heart and life.

Their lovemaking had evolved over the past several years. Winn always made sure that Maureen came, but seemed indifferent to her own orgasm.

Maureen, though, was not indifferent to it. She would return from the deep abyss of her own pleasure to coax and cajole Winn into responding, to seduce and tease her.

Winn would lie back, letting Maureen have her way with her, always cooperative, always pleasant. What Maureen wanted was passion: Winn out of control.

She considered Winn's orgasm both a challenge and a duty. When it came, it was incredibly rewarding.

It was rewarding because of the way it unfolded, layer by layer, sound by sound, quiver by quiver. Maureen could feel it building in the tense thighs warm against her cheeks, in the progressively louder sighs emanating somewhere above her.

She loved to stroke Winn's legs as she made love to her, cradling and kneading the flesh, distracting her lover just a little bit, just a fraction, so that the pleasure could build even more.

Finally she would slide her fingers or a thumb into action along with her tongue, both upper and lower lips, and sometimes her nose or cheekbone.

She loved the moist warmth, the rocking motion, the repetition, the moving meditation of it all.

Winn's climax would announce itself with short, fast, breathless utterances which coincided with a stilled motion in her body. Next would come the forking, lifting motions which tossed Maureen around, forcing her to hold on with determination, to continue licking with a dedicated will.

Winn would lock her fingers in Maureen's hair or scratch her shoulder as she heaved, lovingly, against her face.

Winn was always embarrassed about the scratches later.

Maureen was secretly proud of them, looking in the mirror with satisfaction at the animal hungers she had brought out in her lover, the passion ignited and released.

The colors had dissolved from the sky leaving a silvery grayness lightened and darkened by clouds and mountains. Maureen sang along with the radio, feeling herself deeply connected to and in tune with the car, the road, the passing, sparkling lights, the inky increments of night.

Stars appeared. A gibbous moon rose to her right. She drove on into the night, remembering.

When she reached home, she parked carefully then took the dog for a brief walk. The dog, named Doll Parton, had belonged to Nancy. Winn had inherited her but Maureen had become her truest friend, her fastest buddy.

"Doll, old girl, I may just wake up you-know-who and force her to have sex with me. What do you think of that?"

Doll wagged cheerfully.

The breeze, moist and cool with a hint of rain, wavered across Maureen's body, stirred her hair.

Quietly they reentered the house. Maureen undressed in her own room, brushed, flossed, and washed up slowly, thinking about the sunset, the wind, Winn's hands on her body, Winn's lips and tongue.

She came to their shared bed ripe with anticipation.

"Winn, Winn my love, I'm here," she crooned, spreading herself like butter over her lover's body, melting in.

"I'm so glad you're home," Winn said, sleepily, enfolding Maureen in her arms.

The Long Mirror

Loren had back and neck problems until she learned, at thirty-eight, to masturbate. She learned from reading a book—a very dirty book, with pictures.

Her lover, hot-eyed Janey, was not encouraging.

"I don't understand why you feel you have to masturbate," she said, putting dishes away noisily, banging cupboards and drawers. "Don't we make love enough? Can't I do it for you?" She turned to face Loren who was elbow deep in suds. "And why do you do it standing up, in front of a mirror?"

Loren answered, in dangerously slow measured tones, "Because I saw a photo of someone doing it that way. The image was exciting." She scrubbed at food cooked to the bottom of a pot. "I could *imagine* doing it like the woman in the book. The picture excited me."

"But what about us?"

"It hasn't hurt our sex life any, has it? I love making love with you. This is just different." Sighing, she looked out the window, then back to Janey. "Why won't you understand?"

"Because I don't." Janey stood, a bundle of anger, the dish towel clutched tightly in one fist.

"Then just leave me alone about it, OK?" Loren dried her hands, folded the hand towel and paused at the door, "My back is fine. My neck is fine. My lover is a pain in the ass." She turned and headed into the back yard where she weeded with a vengeance.

As she worked out the tenacious roots, an image of her parents, tight-faced and angry, crossed her mind. She remembered them telling her to get out, that she was an abomination, that they never wanted to see her again. She had never gone back.

Sometimes Janey felt as dogmatic as they were. Yet she genuinely liked Janey, liked the life they'd built: working for the same company, playing volleyball and softball, hosting rowdy gatherings of friends. Janey regularly got involved with rescuing whales or dolphins or seals, raising money or serving as treasurer for one or another of the organizations.

Loren just gardened. "I'm involved with saving us from the poisons they put in store-bought food."

Loren carried the basket of weeds over to the compost pile. She felt like she wanted a cigarette. She remembered the grueling struggle to stop smoking the first year they were together.

Janey had not been kind about her smoking. "Sex is great but kissing you is like licking a dirty ashtray."

Loren's back and neck problems started in their second year. She and Janey had been struggling for some time over Loren's wish to be more out as a lesbian, especially at work.

They had terrible, confrontive fights while Loren canned beets, tomatoes, beans. "Look here, Janey, everyone knows anyway."

Janey glared back at her through the steam. "Maybe they do and maybe they don't. At least they can ignore it now. If you tell them, they'll have to notice."

Loren retreated into silence, her head and neck aching.

Their lovemaking was pleasant enough, but lacked fireworks. Loren often had trouble coming.

50

She tried fantasizing to increase her level of excitement. That helped some. Then she started mail-ordering sex books. Most were about heterosex but some showed women together. Leafing through them, she wasn't sure what she was searching for.

But her pulse would race.

Her chiropractor suggested self-stimulation as a pain reliever for her back. "Sometimes it works better than any prescription drug."

The change in her body had been remarkable. The pain lessened, then went away entirely. There was a change in her mind as well, a sense that she was doing what she had to do, because she had to do it.

She came out, one by one, to all her co-workers. Most of them did know already, but the act was symbolic and opened up the subject for conversation. She learned that several of them had gay relatives about whom they cared deeply. She started looking forward to cafeteria conversations, feeling a new connectedness, a new warmth.

Janey always went out for lunch.

They began to drift apart until Janey, shortly before her fortieth birthday, decided to move out of Loren's house. "I deserve something better than this and, by god, I'm going to find it."

Loren felt sad but relieved. She too started dating, broadened her social activities, sifting and searching for someone special, someone to share her life with.

No one seemed just right.

She continued masturbating, finding in it a pleasure and satisfaction unrelated to sex with a partner. She loved standing in front of the mirror, looking at her body, so different in the daylight, the lamplight, sometimes candlelight.

Loren and Janey remained friends, getting together at least once a week, connecting by telephone and letter. Often they'd talk nostalgically about the good times they'd had as lovers.

Their friends couldn't understand why they'd parted.

One Saturday morning Janey told Loren she'd stopped drinking.

"I didn't know it was a problem," Loren said. "I never saw you drink too much."

"It wasn't the quantity but the way I couldn't socialize without a drink. Anyway, I've stopped. I'm not feeling better, but I think I'm going to."

Janey stayed off booze and started exercising. She began to look more and more the way she had during their first year together, not skinny, but firm and toned, radiant. Sometimes Loren couldn't take her eyes off.

Janey's current lover, Shelley, enjoyed Loren's appreciation of the change in Janey. "I agree," she'd say. "Janey's got a wonderful body." Together they'd ogle her at cook-outs and ball games.

"Cut it out, you two," Janey would say, looking pleased.

Loren had major surgery and didn't know how she was going to manage. Janey and Shelley subleased their apartment, moved in and took care of her during her long convalescence. Loren felt both embarrassed (to be needy) and grateful for their help.

Then Shelley got involved with someone else, (two someones actually), and moved back to the apartment. Janey stayed with Loren.

"Do you want to be lovers again?" Loren asked.

"Not yet," Janey answered and started lifting weights.

They did become lovers again. They'd never stopped loving one another, just lost sight of the love for awhile.

While preparing breakfast one morning, Janey said, "I'm sorry I was so awful about your coming out at work and about the masturbation. It really wasn't any of my business." She pushed her hair back off her forehead with her free hand, stirred the eggs with the other. "I guess I had some pretty rigid ideas about certain things." She shifted from foot to foot. "Anyway, I want to apologize."

Loren put down the grapefruit she had been sectioning, wiped her hands and gathered Janey, spatula and all, into her arms. "Accepted." They kissed until the eggs burned.

Loren scrubbed the fry pan and handed it back to Janey. "Do you want to try doing it together?"

"Doing what?"

"Masturbating."

"Me and my big mouth," Janey said, dropping the margarine on the floor.

"Well," Loren grinned at the usually calm Janey who wouldn't meet her eye.

"Well, all right, I'll try."

They skipped breakfast altogether.

In the bedroom they had shared for so many years Loren pulled the curtains, creating an undersea world of green light, glowing edges. Janey undressed, leaving her tee shirt on and crawled under the covers. Loren did a slow strip before her then turned her back, facing the long mirror. Janey hovered in the mirror beside her, looking tense but grinning anyway.

"So I get to watch, do I?"

"As much as you want."

"What if I can't do it like this, with you right here and all?" Her voice trembled a bit.

"Then we can do it again." Loren smiled a truly wicked grin. "By the third or fourth time it'll probably be easy."

"Me and my big mouth, again," Janey said with a long, exaggerated sigh.

Loren relaxed into her favorite stance, legs slightly spread and bent, forearms snug against the sides of her breasts, both hands cupping her pubic hair, fingers pressing. She began moving her pelvis, the motion controlling the pressure of her fingers. She liked the way she looked: powerful, primeval. She swayed slightly, her pulse dancing, her fingers moist.

It took her a long time to get near climaxing. She just kept going, concentrating on the touch, the warmth of her hands against her body, the spicy smell her body was sending out.

She glanced at Janey in the mirror, seeing her eyes closed, the covers moving. She imagined the responsiveness of that finely muscled body exploding with feelings similar to her own.

Exhilaration raced through her, making her want to shout, to leap and laugh and sing.

As the gulf of pleasure opened for her, sucking her in, she heard the dear, familiar sounds of Janey coming behind her. Her experience was enhanced by the sounds that Janey made.

She threw her head back and added her own voice, became lost in her own sounds, in her own body, flowing.

When the wash of sensation had passed, Loren turned and moved quickly to the bed, diving in, wrapping Janey in her arms and rolling with her.

They laughed uproariously until passion demanded their complete, unwavering attention.

The Island With the Tall Trees

They had met on the island some three years before. Gillian had been thirty, newly out of a confining and oppressive marriage, new to the world of women together. Lonnie had been free of encumberments and entanglements, settling into a caretaker's job which would last through autumn and winter; chopping wood, gathering supplies.

Gillian had her first woman's kiss from Lonnie's lips, her first orgasm through Lonnie's hands.

"Baby, baby," Lonnie had rocked her in her arms, after, as she cried and cried. "Baby, baby, it's all right. It's going to be all right."

"I can't believe I didn't know, all those years."

"I know. It's going to be all right."

Lonnie did seem to know what was going on in those deeper levels of Gillian's being, did connect with her in ways that no one else ever had. Gillian warmed to her, thawed for her, found places in herself that even she hadn't known existed. She told Lonnie everything, anything, held nothing back.

They explored each other's bodies like kids playing, laughing, no taboos.

"I feel so open, like I could go anywhere with you, do anything, and it would be all right," she said.

"You just know how basically conservative, careful and inhibited I am."

"Yes and no. You do know what I mean. I know you do."

Sometimes by the water's edge, bundled in clothing against the wind, they would make love with their hands alone, with the fingertips, the palms, pads, knuckles, backs, rubbing, trailing, dancing, folding and infolding, tugging, pushing, holding, holding, holding.

"I never want to let you go," she said. "I want to hold on tight, hold you forever."

"Spring will come and I'll move on, love. You'll get a job, find out who you are out there in the world. It wouldn't do you any good if I protected you like your husband did. You need to flower, little blossom, to see yourself grow big."

They made love with their lips, soft as puppy ears, kisses like doves wings, like milkweed seeds carried on the wind. Their lips covered each other's body, whispered into the ravines, nibbled in the hollows. They kissed their way out of darkness into the pale of morning, into the brightness of full sunshine.

Lonnie's kisses drew Gillian forward, drew her out of herself, then dropped her back, into, inside, deeper and deeper into the essence of who she was, she who had been hidden from herself.

The autumn leaves swept across the pine needles, banked against the cabin. Deciduous trees stood naked and exposed.

"My soul's exposed to you. My heart and soul. I didn't know love could be like this."

"Love can be so many ways. It's always a surprise."

They made love with their hands under the covers, under their clothes, reaching and touching and feeling, following each move the other made. It was like the sweep of the wind swaying the trees, wailing and moaning, the trees moving in an intimate call and response.

They made love with their hands, cupping and wrapping and holding and listening. They were lesbians together, loving in those age-old ways that women do.

They made love with words, talking each other into excitement, into satisfaction, into satiation.

Their whole bodies made love each to the other, flowing over one another like water over rocks, blending and merging, fitting together with exquisite precision.

Snow came, blanketing the world with a silence so profound they echoed it, not talking for days, sensing each other, following one another. Loving.

Their loving deepened yet again. Gillian could feel her womb contract when she came, could feel her toes curl, her skin expand, her heart burst open.

As the thaws began, she began pulling back, contracting, building walls against the coming pain.

They separated on the first day of spring.

Now, three years later, they're going to see each other again. The island hasn't changed, the tall trees sway with measured grandeur. Gillian is aware of her own growth, her enlarged world view, the confidence she has gained in herself.

For three years, though, there has been a dull ache in a small, quiet corner of her being. Who is it that Lonnie has become? Is the person she knew still there or gone forever? Why has she even agreed to meet this way? What good can possibly come of it?

Lonnie arrives in a jeep, the wheels a little muddy, the sides splashed, a license plate that reads IM HERE.

The wind whispers loudly in the vacancy left as the engine quiets. Lonnie opens the door, but stays inside, watching her. Gillian starts running, her body knowing before her mind just where she wants to be, who she wants to be with.

Jennifer's Song

It's early morning on the first day of autumn and Jennifer is walking in the mountains north of San Francisco. Far below to her right the North Bay spreads and sparkles. The path winds gently through low brush and grasses, passes rapidly beneath her rhythmic long stride.

She has just broken up with a lover of six years, a relationship full of grand excesses and decided problems which became more distressing with each passing year. Today she wants to say goodbye, inside herself, to all the good qualities that she had loved in the other. She also wants to forgive herself for staying so long, for holding onto the familiar despite her growing pain.

The pain had made her stretch and grow, she acknowledges, but the pleasure had been greater during most of those years. She meditates on the pleasure, her body remembering details that her conscious mind had forgotten.

Jennifer is wearing shorts, a white shirt, lightweight jacket, prescription sunglasses, and chartreuse running shoes. The running shoes are new. She carries a bottle of lemon-flavored water, sandwiches, and carrots. She had sprayed herself with perfume just before leaving her new home. Now she smells that exciting, familiar scent she has worn so often for others. She hums as she walks.

Everything had happened so fast: the decision, the breakup, the movers, crying for hours in her old lover's arms, even making love one last time. Twice. She thinks about the beloved's body, warm, moist, fragrant, elusively available. Sometimes the other wouldn't come at all or, starting to respond, would suddenly want to go out to dinner, go for a walk, finish a project. Life in general had fluctuated too. Jennifer never knew to whom she would come home.

She had treasured the changeability, her lover's mercurial temperament, for its difference from her repressed and orderly childhood. They'd made love on the living room floor, the kitchen table, under the bed, in the bathroom, under bushes, clinging to trees. Jennifer, who had trouble with orgasms in the past, found she could come at will, quivered whenever they came in contact, rushed off at times to masturbate and relieve her overflowing tension.

Masturbation had come late for her and sometimes still was scary. Her lover always encouraged her, would hold her saying, "Touch yourself. Please. Touch yourself for me." Jennifer laughs now, remembering her embarrassment. Her sexuality had expanded as she touched herself, learned to give herself pleasure instead of always expecting it from someone else.

Whenever they made love her beloved had taken great pleasure in watching her react, had delighted in her uneven breath, electrified flesh. Jennifer would want to hurry, to say, "Down there. Touch me down there, now."

Her lover almost always made love slowly, deliberately, watching, eyes sparkling.

Jennifer would cry out as she came. Her lover called this utterance "singing," commented about it later in the day, sometimes for days following. "You sang loud and clear that time," or "I loved the way you sang yesterday," pause, "with a little catch in your voice."

She begins singing now as she walks the hard-packed earth. The song is tuneless, single notes thrown out and held until they fade. It rises somewhere deep inside her body in a tingling, sexual way. She varies the tone, finds that her shoulders respond to one note, her tits to another, and her clit seems to notice everything, including the tightness of her pants, the rhythmical rubbing of her shorts.

The sounds she's making, gong-like, incantatory, roll up and out of her, leaving oscillating rivulets in their wake. A hawk circles. She removes her jacket and ties it around her shoulders. Mist, caught in green pockets, drifts toward her. The early morning odors change with the warmth, becoming musky, then sultry. Her perfume intensifies. Her pulse drums with excitement.

She locates a knoll isolated above the path and settles her food about her. In the far distance a blue, translucent San Francisco shimmers. The sandwich is egg salad, the egg cut in large chunks, pungent with garlic, mustard, basil, and onion. The bread is whole wheat, dark and fragrant, cut in quarters.

As she eats she remembers her old lover's passion for her cooking: "Jennifer can make anything taste superb."

She must become passionate about herself now, pay attention to her own most intimate desires. Slowly and with great intensity she finishes the sandwich, licks mayo from her fingers, drinks some water, spilling drops against her chin, against her chest. She smells her own heat rising, mixing with the lemon, with her perfume.

She remembers her lover's sense of need, her own wild hungers, nights when they seemed to devour each other, the smells of sex lingering on their bodies, permeating the cooling air. She smiles, thinking of herself as her own lover, her own best friend.

She smiles, opens her mouth wider, draws deeper breaths into her lungs. She feels forgiveness rising with the other sensations, thankfulness rising. She can forgive the other, can finally forgive herself.

With a finely deliberate motion she reaches down and opens her pants. Reaching in, she touches herself between her legs.

She finds her vulva swollen and responsive, the small clit-head alive with sensations. She sighs and rubs, reaching further to test the moisture, raising her fingers to smell the ripeness. She reaches down and in to pull and spread the liquid, squeeze and press. Her fingers move in all the old and favored ways.

She thinks, "This is what I want," as she touches herself repeatedly, lovingly, teasingly, demandingly.

Another hawk appears making lazy, circles in the cloudless sky. As the bird circles, her eyes follow, then her body, circling, rising. When she starts to come, she drops her eyes, beginning a new love song with San Francisco glowing between her legs.

She leans her head back, her face to the sun. Tendons taut, her chest expands as sound fills her, flows out of her.

The sound continues for a long time. Even after her call has ended, it echoes within her head, within her flesh, shaking her bones.

The air is very still.

Eyes closed, she sits and cries, holding herself, rocking. In time her awareness returns slowly to her body, to the trees and brush around her, to the mountain beneath.

The hawk is gone, the sky and city brighter, the earth smells midday hot. Humming, she arranges her clothing, gathers her belongings, and returns to the winding path.

Fast Cars and Fast Women

"I like fast cars and fast women," she said, and I got in.

Movement was the metaphor for our connection: black-top moving under the wheels, under our running shoes, wind thrusting against us. Wind billowed the catamaran's sails and sent foaming whitecaps jumping across the waves, salt spray across our bodies.

Snow flew as we turned with the long skis. It swept out from us in acres of white on cross-country trips, faster, faster, sun goggles in place, the chill of exhilaration in my nose, in my mouth.

The smell of speed, of excitement, permeated my life.

"I'm not young any more, thank God," she said. "I'm in my prime."

"And primed," I'd say and then I'd grin at her and we'd be off again with tickets to some sporting event or gay society bonanza.

"You look stunning," she'd say, pausing, one hand in her jacket pocket, looking me up and down.

I loved constructing myself as an object of her desire; the shopping and planning and dressing, the thrill of her attention. I'd paint my nails while listening to a favorite album repeat in quadraphonic sound, the subtle rhythms caressing me like a hypnotic induction. Each stroke of color added a layer of memory, recreating situations and environments in which we had been together.

Strauss would leap out toward me from a compact disk as I inhaled the enamel odor, so much a part of this ritual activity. I always feel her hands upon me when the *Blue Danube* plays or *Roses From the South*, her hands firmly and definitively leading me through the gracious swaying of one waltz after another.

Later I'd soak in the fragrant mineral salted water, lights dimmed, the air redolent of lavender and roses. I'd dry myself slowly, touching my body with love, indulging in all the joys of preparation, of anticipation.

She took time with her own looks as well, the tailoring, folding, pressing were all done with a care that belied her casual, sporty appearance. Men as well as other women found her attractive, turned and smiled at her, deferred to her, moved with her in slow, courting ways even though they knew she was unavailable.

She always let me know that I was the subject of her passion. She let all others know as well.

Seasons came and crested. Her hand would graze my cheek or breast or thigh. Her fingers light and firm would linger on my body, linger in my memory, transport and thrill me, calm and console me.

She touched other areas of my life as well, encouraging, explaining, unfolding possibilities. I was older than she, but much more naive, psychologically younger, less worldly, when we met.

"Don't invest in that company. They look good now but their CEO has a weakness for coke. Try any of these instead. They're growing more slowly but they'll pay more in the long run."

"Try a bit of this," she'd say, holding out a bite of brie, escargot, sashimi, marinated I-don't-know-what. And I would, closing my eyes and concentrating on the flavors, the blending, the texture, the after-taste. There was always more. It was rather like learning to make love, a deepening and unfolding in layers, over time, always more.

She cooked elegantly, treating me to candlelit dinners of grilled fresh fish, stuffed mushrooms, steamed artichokes, baked pears in a delicate sauce, tiny beet-pickled eggs. She served the most incredibly delicious moist chocolate cake, but only on the rarest of occasions. "I never want to take it for granted," she'd say, measuring carefully. "Complacency is death to the senses."

On the spur of the moment she'd take me joy riding, whisking me up to see a particularly spectacular view of some city or the layers of a valley, or the way the waves crashed against the shore.

"Hang on," she'd say, rounding a mountain curve, creating a sharp angle in the snow, negotiating white water on one of the world's magnificent rivers.

"Let's go," she'd say, taking my elbow, steering me into warm, sunny days and glittering, joy-filled nights.

She always wore her seat belt, made me wear one too. "I like speed, but I like my brains as well. Want to keep them in my head."

I'd learned at home to love glamour, speed and style, but it had always gone along with recklessness before. She gave me the excitement without the alcoholic brawls.

"Alcohol doesn't like me," she'd say, toasting with seltzer and lime. "It just comes right back up whenever I try. And believe me, I've tried."

But there was more to it than that.

She didn't smoke or sniff or shoot things into her veins. "Ugh," she'd say. "They'd slow me down."

"Come on," she'd say, striding to the car door which she'd open with a flourish.

"Grab the food," she'd say, unwinding the docking ropes and pushing off.

"Come on," she'd say as I straddled her, her fingers inside me, her thumb on my clit. "Come on, my sleek lady lion," her finger in my ass, her hand on my breast. "Come, let me eat you," she'd murmur as she nuzzled into my fur. "Come for me," she'd call and pull me into

64

the air, my legs over her shoulders, my hands touching my own nipples.

And I would.

We'd speed along springtime roads banked with dogwood, autumn highways maple-splashed or elegant with aspen gold.

"No regrets," she'd say, shifting the car into fourth, acceleration pushing me against the leather, laughing.

"No regrets," I'd say, as she pushed me against the seat, against soft rugs, into lush bedding.

Sometimes she'd become so turned on she couldn't wait until we found a safe place, a motel, our home.

"Take me now, here, fast," she'd say and I'd reach into her pants to find her moist, ready, vibrating. And then she'd cry out as she'd come once, twice, sometimes even three times, "Aarouuuuu," a sound like a lone wolf calling to the moon.

Why we were never caught I still don't know. Perhaps because it happened so fast and then we were gone, driving or jogging or skiing, laughing with pleasure.

It's happening still. Our passion has flashed for years now. I don't know how or if it will end. She loves the speed and I'm along for the ride.

River Trip

It was a glorious day to be out on the river. The morning sun hung poised just above the treetops.
A flawless sky was criss-crossed by graceful, slow-wheeling birds. Massive cliffs reached straight up, patterned with lichen, dotted with small yellow flowers.

Deena and Lou had promised themselves a river trip for years. They now shared a large, orange raft-boat with four other women and a guide.

They approached the first rapids cautiously. Deena glanced across at Lou, whose face was filled with a fierce concentration. Lou looked back at her, held her glance with the level stare of love, raised one eyebrow in the teasing, daring way she used to do, before work and familiarity created comfortable ruts for them to slide into.

They'd been through so much together, come out together, gotten sober together. They weren't just workaholics, they were sober alcoholics. No one, though, had been around to teach them how to have sex without the drinking.

Deena loved this strong, attractive, competent woman. She wished, oh, she wasn't quite sure what, that they could be closer somehow, touch more, love more.
Moment by moment the tumbling roar of the water grew.

She let go of Lou's eyes, hoping that the intensity of her caring had leaped the space between them. She dug

66

her paddle in, chanting "love, love, love," into the rushing wind, into the morning air.

Before her lay a shifting expanse of rippling foam and whirling eddies, sparkling in the morning sun, roaring all around her. The boat jerked and bucked. Spray crashed over the bow, causing the two in the front to cry out and lift their paddles, to almost lose their balance.

"Dig in! Dig in!" the guide cried. "Don't raise your paddles! Dig in." They crested a wave, then turned sideways, sliding and splashing down a sharp, rapid swirl, paddling hard to straighten the boat out.

Deena laughed with the joy of it, her heart pounding with fear and love.

"Left, back," the guide called and Deena pushed down and held to the limit of her strength, watching as the maneuver pulled them gracefully back on course.

"All paddle now," and Deena reached out again, feeling powerful and vibrantly alive, pleased with herself, expansive toward the world.

On reaching calmer waters, Deena looked around at the canyon live oaks clinging to the dry grassy slopes, at the osprey and turtles and crows. A fish almost jumped into the boat.

She wished she could find a way to carry this aliveness, this heightened perception back into their home. Sex was pleasant, but rare and oh, so predictable.

She noticed the smell of something dead, returning itself to the soil. She loved those cycles of nature, even the harsh smells, the pungent smells had a beauty, when she could just relax into them, notice them without tensing against them.

It was rather like the smell of sex, learning to like it by relaxing into it, letting it become part of her, flow through her. Lou always wanted to wash up before and after, hated to linger in bed smelling like "over-ripe fruit." Maybe that could change, though. She'd never tried to talk about it with her.

More rapids appeared around a bend. The tumbling water seemed to reach for the little boat, roaring its siren song, promising excitement as well as danger. The white water threw them up, then caught and pulled them down and forward and up again. "It's like loving, all day loving, without ever really coming," she thought, understanding for the first time about the "river rats," those men and a few women who live only for the time they can spend on the water, taking their last trips of the year in December and their first in January, no matter what the weather is like.

They were swept into the calm of another canyon, blue and yellow-orange flowers making a feathery display along the steep, chunky walls.

Deena looked at Lou, attractive even in the bulk of life-vest. She loved her, loved her dearly, deeply. Couldn't imagine living without her, living with anyone else. Somehow their teaching jobs and the upkeep around their aging home kept them from spending much special time together. They did go out to dinner fairly regularly but the candlelight was gone, the stars and mushy music were gone. Could they possibly get it back?

The water flowed swift and deep, carrying them casually on its back. A light breeze gently caressed her face. Spray had dried from her skin and now the sun was warm upon her. She waved away an insistent fly.

Before sobriety, sex had been wonderful and easy, she just couldn't remember much about it. Now she remembered everything, there just wasn't much to remember.

Deena looked at Lou again. Lou was flushed, smiling broadly back at her, the old Lou, quirky and fun-loving, holding that dykey eye contact until the overt sexuality of it almost made her squirm. Deena wondered if Lou's thoughts had been taking the same kind of direction as her own.

They ate lunch on a sandy bank backed by willows and towering cliffs, then stretched out in the hot sand.

"This feels terrific," Deena said, inching her shoulder toward Lou's.

"And you looked positively edible out there on the river, sweetheart," Lou murmured back.

"I'll take you up on that at the earliest possible moment."

"Promise?"

"Yeah."

Deena lay beside her lover, almost shockingly aware of the slight arm contact, that place where their edges merged. What could she do to carry this excitement back home to bed? She no longer believed that it would work itself out in time. Perhaps talking about it would help but that was terribly scary.

On the river again, they coasted for what seemed like a long time, soaking up the sun, twisting along the mossy banks and spectacular views.

"We're coming to a big one, now. It's the last of the trip. Remember, don't raise your arms. Keep paddling no matter what. If you fall in, get your feet up - nose and toes up, pointing downstream."

Deena shot a final passionate look at Lou then wrenched her eyes back to the water breaking over submerged rocks. The roar filled her ears, echoed in her blood.

She paddled as if her life depended on it. There was no time now to look around, to take in the color and swirl of the water, the land beyond. She kept her eyes focused on the pacesetter in front, matching her stroke for stroke.

Waves seemed to be hitting them from both sides, jerking and bucking the little craft around. More than once Deena lost her balance and slid to the center of the boat, then rushed to pull herself into her position again, wedge in her feet and paddle, paddle, turning the flat side to slip it through the air and pushing it down and in again.

Intense buffeting jarred the little craft. Deena sensed

more than saw Lou go over the side into a mass of milky foam.

Terror swept through Deena. It was her job, as the person opposite Lou, to get her lover back into the boat. The possibility of losing Lou, of losing their life together, suddenly swept over her. She slid across the wet rubber flooring and reached out with her paddle, seeing Lou so close, carried along at the same rate that the boat was traveling, flailing with one hand, her paddle in the other. Lou got hold of the paddle, then lost her grip as a wave pulled them around a bend, crashed over her head, held her under.

Deena prayed for help, for strength.

Lou broke water again and grabbed twice for the paddle before catching it. Deena pulled her to the side of the boat. Securing both paddles, she grabbed her lover's life jacket from behind. Her fear said, "Hurry," while another voice in her head reviewed the earlier instructions. She pushed down and pulled up in a bouncing motion three times before standing, clutching her lover to her and falling, falling with her backward into the boat, a tangle of arms and legs. Everyone cheered.

"You did it perfectly, right by the book!" The guide called.

Deena rested, shock and exhaustion rushing through her. She squeezed Lou's arms, so thankful to have her back in the boat, back against her.

"I love you," she whispered, feeling the words inadequate to express the total relief she felt, the total commitment to this familiar, beloved woman. She gave a little extra squeeze and then a push to help Lou off of her. They took up their paddles and turned again to the rushing, foaming, crashing waters.

Deena started shaking, calmed herself with the knowledge that this was her body's way of balancing itself after the ordeal.

They were coming out of the rapids now, entering a broad expanse of calm. Awareness of what they had survived together was growing in Deena, deepening her commitment to this union, her determination to talk about their problems, to work things out.

That night they lay before the fire, achy, drowsy, well fed.

"Sweet Deena, you know when I thought I might die out there, I felt angry, like we'd been missing something together. I mean, it's a good life we have but, I don't know. It's like it's all on the surface, on top of the water, and there's a lot beneath that we haven't explored very much. Am I making any sense to you?"

"Yes love, yes you are."

"Well, I was thinking about sex before I went over."

"Me too."

"And I think we need to do something about the way we, you know, the way, well," she reached for a mug of spiced cider, "the way — Hell, I can't even talk about it!"

"I understand." Deena held and stroked Lou, glad that she hadn't had to bring it up after all.

"Anyway, maybe we could read some books together, or get some videos to watch, or go get some counseling." Lou unbuttoned Deena's shirt and reached inside.

"Or all of those." Deena closed her eyes, appreciating the warmth against her flesh.

"Right. What do you think?" Lou kissed Deena's forehead, following the hairline, the smooth, warm lips leaving a fiery trail in their wake. She moved to Deena's neck, to the opening in her shirt.

"Hummm, great ideas. I remember the speakers I've heard who talked about how hard sex was after sobriety." She rubbed her face in Lou's hair, liking the fresh washed smell of it, the crispy curls of it. "I always thought we handled it pretty well, but I don't think that any more." Reaching down she massaged Lou's neck, encouraging her to go on.

71

"I feel like, well, like I've been missing a part of myself and that all the work and the house and yard just covered up that other need." She took a deep breath and sighed. "Maybe I don't even know how to do sex without drinking."

Lou had Deena's shirt completely open now. She pulled the shirttail free and kissed and sucked each nipple in turn then continued rubbing them as she turned her face up to Deena's. "But maybe we can find out how or figure it out. I'd like to try."

The sensations in Deena's breasts spread like hot honey, flowed outward and downward warming her belly and the regions beyond. She remembered this feeling from long ago and now relaxed into it, letting it flow through her, take her wherever it would. "Lou, oh Lou, yes, please, yes."

Songbird

Keiko Alberti slipped quietly into her father's night-club, The Glorious Gate. She had come to help celebrate his birthday, to make common bond with the only family she had, the person she loved more than any other in the world. He was the only one who had always been there for her.

Keiko paused in front of a wall of mirrors, smoothed the silken cloth of her black dress, the smooth cap of her dark hair. She still looked eighteen instead of twenty-seven but the formal dress added maturity and elegance. In the sound studio at work she was often mistaken for a kid, an illusion quickly shattered by watching her work.

She looked terrific even if she did feel out of sorts. She wasn't sure what her discomfort was all about. She thought, perhaps, she was feeling sorry for herself for not having a steady lover although no one had really interested her in a couple of years. She thought she was beyond feeling sorry for being queer, for having a queer father, for her mother's early death. She thought again of going to Japan to look for her mother's family but decided not yet, maybe never.

It was early. Her favorite seat at the end of the bar was still vacant. She liked to settle there where she could see the whole room.

"What'll it be, little mama?" Jason asked, wiping

down the bar in front of her and settling a napkin with elaborate flourish.

"How about a Shirley Temple, Jason? Maybe it will cheer me up."

"Whatever it takes, honey, I'm on your side."

Keiko sipped the sweet blend of fruit juice and seltzer, so familiar from her childhood. She watched the band set up and tune their instruments. She'd heard they were good.

They brought back her days as a lead singer and sometimes bass player in a small-time dance band. The leader had called her their exotic canary. She'd loved the music, the attention and, after they were better known, the good money she was making.

She got fired because too many lesbians were coming in, sitting down front, beaming at her.

"Get rid of them," the leader said.

"But I don't even know them."

"They know you're gay, that's why they're here."

"Fuck you," she said after one of these encounters. And that was it, on her own again after two years of thinking she knew who she was, where she belonged.

She looked around the nightclub, admiring the lush potted plants, each illuminated by its own grow light, each a testament to her father's loving care. She wished she could flower as easily for him as the plants did. She drank a little more from the still frosty glass.

It wasn't long after she had gotten fired that she was asked to sing in a women's band, one that played in lesbian bars and for women only dances.

That's where Keiko met Arlie, Arleen Dunsmuir with the river dark eyes and the moaning pedal steel guitar. Arlie's fingers would play the strings all evening and Keiko's body until daylight. They experimented with sex like music, playing variations, learning new melodies, new harmonies. Always, though, at dawn, Arlie would come against her face, would come and cry and Keiko would then hold her until they both fell asleep.

74

"Why do you cry, you know, after?" she asked her early on.

"It's just so real, so, I don't know, so overwhelming."

Sometimes they sang together, interweaving their voices in an erotic incantation, in a public display of seduction and desire.

In private Keiko felt the songs run through her body, felt the loving, caring magic open her up, open new doors for her, whole new worlds of experience.

Keiko learned sound engineering in order to work on the band's first record, layering and augmenting the music in an intense, obsessed act of love.

Shortly after the record was released she saw Arlie making love, backstage, with the newest member of the band.

She watched for quite awhile, stunned and shaken, then she had wandered the afternoon streets for hours, vague, disoriented. She found Arlie at the apartment when she got home.

"I saw you with Gina today."

"Yes?" Arlie finished putting a record on the turntable and turned to face her. "So? It didn't mean anything. She's a nice kid, sort of lonely, you know."

"Didn't mean anything? Didn't mean anything? What does? What does mean something to you? I certainly don't." Keiko looked around in her anger, looked for something to throw, to hit, to hurt. Grabbing Arlie's instrument she flung it against the doorjamb, hearing the snapping, breaking sounds as an echo of her heart.

Keiko sat then and cried, cried for all the loses she'd ever had, cried for the dreams smashed like the instrument, smashed, dissolved, muddied, gone.

When Arlie tried to talk with her, to comfort her, Keiko pushed her away. "Just leave me alone. I hurt."

Arlie went away and Keiko packed, crying, talking softly to herself. She left an envelope with a check for the guitar pinned to Arlie's pillow.

So long ago now, five years at least, the pain was almost gone but memories of the loving, of the good and sexy times, still came back to stir her to melancholy.

"Hi sugar," Her father's voice slipped gently into her memories.

She dropped the troubling past immediately and smiled at him, noticing the finely tailored suit, neat graying hair, his faintly swishy, faintly ironic dignity. A handsome hunk, they called him, a handsome hunk of a sweet daddy-o. He kissed her on each cheek then leaned back, looking at her admiringly.

"Will you sing for me tonight, sugar?"

"You know I will."

"Later then," he squeezed her hand and left to greet the regulars, welcome newcomers, give this colorful arboretum the intimacy of a best friend's living room.

"What's up, little mama?" Jason asked, wiping the bar and holding up her empty glass.

"Oh give me a seltzer and lime this time. I'm just stuck in the past, Jason, remembering the past."

"Again? Honey don't you know it's time for you to sparkle up to someone new? Anybody will do for a starter. Dance a little, shimmy a little. Pretend you're having fun and you'll draw the real thing to you."

"I know, Jason. I'm just looking for the right someone."

"Just about any someone can be right if you give them a chance."

"Not for me, Jason. Not for me."

"Ha," Jason moved gracefully down the bar to wait on a new customer, then another.

Keiko turned to see an all too familiar figure separating from the crowd and moving toward her. Her first response was to deny reality, this just could not, should not, be happening.

"There you are," Arlie said, standing before her, handsome as ever. "I've been looking for you."

"What are you doing here?"

"Like I said. Looking for you, Kea."

"This can't be good."

"Keiko, listen to me." Arlie's hands held her shoulders: warm hands, strong, firm. Her face was terribly serious and close, so close. Flashes from the past overlaid the present.

"Listen to me, please, we need your help. The band's got to cut a new record." Arlie let go of her shoulders, leaving a void where her hands had been. Keiko struggled to follow her words, but wanted to reach out and touch her face instead.

She looked away, searching for calm. Her body let her know, loudly, that the old fires still burned.

"Kea, please. Our lead singer just got herself in a wreck. She's not going to get better." Arlie ran a hand through her hair. "I've wanted you back for a long time, but damnit, my pride kept holding me back." Her eyes held Keiko now, level, smoky. "I need you. We all need you."

"Jesus, Arlie, I don't know." Keiko ran a hand over her hair and down to the back of her neck. "I was just thinking about you, about us." She reached for her drink, trying to clear her mind.

"I think about you all the time. Have for years. Half the songs on the new album I wrote to you." Arlie just stood there, filling her vision. "Think about it, please. I'm awfully sorry about what happened. Listen Kea, I love you. I love you, still."

Keiko didn't know what to say. A multitude of voices seemed to be talking inside her head.

"I'll be over there, near the stage, all evening. Here's where I'm staying. Listen, I won't ask anything else of you, just come make beautiful music with me, again. Please."

A hand appeared on Arlie's shoulder, gently moving her aside.

77

"Hello, there," Keiko's father appeared, looking questioningly from one to the other.

"This is Arlie, Dad, the one whose guitar I smashed."

"The fool who didn't treat your daughter right is more like it. Glad to meet you, sir."

Keiko took Arlie's hand, a decision forming and firming. "Dad, Arlie's cutting a new record soon. She's asked me to sing with her on it." Keiko looked searchingly at Arlie's face then back to her father's. She reached out and took a hand of each of these beloved people. "I'm going to do it."

Vibrator Party

"Come on Ali. Don't you want to go just a little bit? Just to see what it's like?" Dale fiddled with the remnants of her croissant, eyes twinkling under her dark eyebrows, auburn hair curling just above the top of her collar.

"A vibrator party? Doing it with other people around? I don't think I could." Ali brought the coffee pot over and filled both mugs, savoring the smell. She looked at her friend, who glowed in a splash of morning sunlight. "No. I just don't think I could." She shook her head as she spoke, replacing the pot on the burner. Moving into the sunlight, she massaged Dale's shoulders through her plaid shirt. Those muscles were always tight from work and enthusiasm. "How many people did you say were invited?"

"Twenty." Dale stirred the coffee to cool it, raised the cup and inhaled deeply. "You make the best coffee in town."

"It's the cinnamon, I always tell you. You could add it to your own at home." She presses deeply with her thumbs.

"The scenery's better here. Anyway, about the party, you have to bring food to share and, of course, your own vibrator. And a towel for the hot tub."

"Hot tub? I haven't been in a hot tub with anyone around since, well, you know, since the surgery." Ali worked her way down Dale's backbone and under her shoulder blades. "And what would I do about clothing during the — would you call it 'sex' time?"

"I'm calling it an orgy and you could leave them on. Why don't you wear a tee shirt in the hot tub if you don't want people to see. Lots of the women who'll be there know about your operation. They won't mind. And if they do, it's their own problem." She drank some coffee then leaned back into Ali's fingers.

"You're serious about this, aren't you?"

"You bet, pal. You've been a turtle for far too long. I remember the days when you had a new lover every year and a few extras in between, like for special occasions. You liked sex and you liked variety." Dale's hand stroked the warm mug. "Then, when they told you that you had cancer, you quit, cold. That was it." She took another long drink.

"But my body was so pretty then, Dale. It's not any more." Ali refilled Dale's cup then leaned against the counter.

Dale's eyes held her. "Your insides are pretty. That's what people always like about you. And you're brave, too, always have been. Where's the woman who used to jump out of planes with me? Who surfed with me when we were in college? Who learned hang gliding when she was forty?"

She's forty-five and missing some of her chest and very self-conscious. That's where she is." Ali felt herself drawing back. She crossed her arms against her friend. "Don't you understand? I'm afraid I'll make people sick. I'll ruin the party just by being there."

Ali turned abruptly to the sink and splashed cold water on her face. She was shaking. She wanted to go to the party. It was just . . . she was so afraid. She dried her face, picked up her well-cooled coffee and sat down. The sun had moved a bit. Its warmth felt good against the cold inside her.

"It's not a gathering of tender shoots, you know. We all have to deal with changes in our bodies. Some of us

80

just have scars that don't show." Dale looked out the window, her jaw tight.

Ali remembered Dale telling of the beatings her father gave her as a kid, strapping her with a belt, calling it discipline. And those beatings had left marks inside. Dale never let anyone get very close. Ali had known her a long time and knew that those barriers were dense. She reached across and covered Dale's hand with her own.

"I know, hon. Something's hard for everyone. It's just that sex was always easy for me. Now, I feel like I have to learn all over again and maybe," she took a long drink, "maybe, it's so hard, it's just not worth it."

"Try it, you might like it," Dale said with a growl and a leer.

Ali laughed. "Okay. Okay. I'll think about it."

Arriving a little late for the party, Ali hoped she looked calmer than she felt.

"I'm still not sure this is a good thing to do." Ali carried a bag containing smoked oysters, miniature corn, olives, pickles, paté, and crackers, and her overnight case. Dale had both sleeping bags, pillows, and a knapsack. Ali glanced at her as they climbed the stairs into the old Victorian. She would be brave for herself as well as for Dale. She didn't have to do anything she didn't want to. She could hang out in the kitchen or watch videos or climb into her sleeping bag and go to sleep. Sleep? Would she be able to sleep, or, if she participated, would she be able to climax? Hell, could she even plug it in? Could she bear to look at other women with both their breasts?

She rang the bell.

"Welcome." Lena, smiling warmly, swung the door wide wearing a flowery, elegant caftan. Her hair a pale pink-orange spray around her head. "Settle your gear in the third room on the left. The kitchen's on down the hall. Hot tub's out back."

Shortly, Ali sat in what must have once been a bedroom. Now the floor was covered wall-to-wall with foam

81

pads topped by patterned rugs. Electrical outlets were prominent above the baseboards. Lighting was low. On the walls were enlargements of old pornographic pictures, pastel tinted views of women together in and out of turn-of-the-century garb. Ali had seen their like before but always small, in books. She stared now, wondering what the women's lives had been like. Were they happy? Well-paid? What happened when they reached middle age? She wished some of them had scars.

"Hi, pal. Dreaming?" Dale, wearing a terry robe, leaned against the door.

"I used to look like that, only skinnier. I wish I'd had some pictures taken. You know, before." Ali finished unrolling her sleeping bag, then took her vibrator and abruptly plugged it into the nearest socket. Turning to her friend, she raised her chin and took a deep breath.

"Dale . . ."

"You're doing fine, pal, just fine. And looking great. No one can tell if the glitter in your eyes is terror or excitement."

A recording of *We've Come A Long, Long Way* played in the distance. It was true she'd come a long, long way. Just getting this far, to this house, this room, had taken so much. Could she go that further distance to the hot tub and, beyond that, party later in this room?

She undressed down to a tank top that said IT'S A NATU-RAL, put on her kimono and followed Dale down the hall, her heart banging around as if her chest were hollow.

"Dale, I'm just not sure." She pulled at the back of her friend's robe.

Turning, Dale gathered her into her arms, snug but not tight.

"Here. Rest a minute. We can go as slow as you like."

Ali's face pressed against the soft, worn robe. She inhaled the fresh, minty smell, the soap and cologne smells, inhaled safety, familiarity.

"Hey, you two, since when were you an item?" Joani slapped Dale on the butt, squeezed Ali's arm. "I'm jealous." Ali stared at Joani's ample body, unclothed and unmarked.

"We're not," Dale said. There was a flatness in her voice. Joani was one of Dale's ex-lovers.

"Well, well, who knows what's next?" Joani waved and headed into the bathroom.

Ali laughed, feeling the tension wash out of her. She'd known Dale longer than anyone else in her life now.

"God, we've been friends for more than thirty years!"

"I know. I don't think about it much. Makes me think I'm older than I feel." Dale put her arm around Ali in a protective way, encouraging her down the hall, staying beside her out onto the deck where all Ali could see was flesh and more flesh. Panic. Women stretched out sunbathing, giving and receiving back rubs, playing ping-pong. No one had a stitch on.

"I wish I wore glasses so I could take them off," she muttered.

Slowly her fear subsided as she recognized most of the faces even though she couldn't put names to them all. Several people waved.

"Hi, Dale."

"Hi, Ali."

"There's juice and wine on the table. Don't pee in the tub."

"Ah, there you are." Lena was submerged with several other women in the large redwood tub. She climbed out, wrapping a large towel around her waist. Ali's breath caught midway down her throat. All she could see was Lena's chest with its one full, tanned breast and the flattened curve where the other had once been, the smoothness divided by a pale, uneven scar.

With great effort Ali raised her eyes to Lena's face.

"How did you learn to be so open about . . . so calm about . . . ?" Her eyes dropped their question to the scarred line. "I've never seen anyone else's." Her hand rose and fell back.

"Do you want to touch?"

The world seemed absolutely still and very bright. The ping-pong ball resounded hollowly. A plane dully roared overhead. A yellow jacket buzzed Ali's face. Absently she waved it away.

Her pulse was very loud inside her.

Ali searched Lena's face for any hesitation and found there a quiet strength, passive, waiting.

"Yes I do want to touch." She raised her hand and lightly stroked the warm flesh, tracing the seam from end to end, then resting the back of her hand against it.

She smiled at Lena. "You're very brave."

"Arrogant too. I decided I didn't want to be cut off from my own life, from so many of the things I enjoy. My first time at a nude beach was hard, but no one paid very much attention."

Dale squeezed her shoulder. "I'm going to get some juice. Want anything?"

"Some wine with, I don't know, maybe a strawberry or something."

All around her conversations were continuing. Ali felt hot all over. Her own fear was a sharp odor in her nostrils, fear and something else . . . excitement?

Quickly she dropped her kimono and pulled the tank top over her head.

"So yours run that way." Lena traced the dual lines inward. "When?"

"Two years ago."

Lena nodded as if taking in the whole complex surrounding the operation: the worry and anger, the sense of loss and mutilation, the shame.

"Any recurrence?"

"None so far."

Dale came back with two plastic glasses, cherries and raspberries in the light wine.

Ali took the cup, her hand shaking slightly. "Did you know this would happen?"

"I knew nothing would change if you stayed at home, old pal." Dale quickly brushed her fingers across Ali's lips and cheek.

"Come. Join us." Lena gestured toward the tub.

Ali turned and began the long, celebratory walk across the deck, Lena on one side, Dale on the other.

A murmur of voices, sighs, and groans hovered around the room, mingling with recorded music, with the smell of flowers, of musk.

Indistinct figures moved in the gentle, warm light, sometimes crossing the video screen on which two women were going down on each other.

Ali exhaled an exasperated sigh. "I just can't come." She turned off the Hatachi's motor and shifted her position, smoothing her maroon nightgown.

Dale, half-tucked into a sleeping bag next to her, clicked off her antiquated Oster and turned from the video.

"Want some help, pal?"

"Or some from me?" Lena, her loose robe open, knelt beside Ali, a tin of oysters in her hand. "Here, try one of these."

Ali ate without thinking, then focused on the warm, heavy flavor, eating from Lena's fingers, sucking the juice. The buttery, smoky smell reminded her of being a child at adult parties, sampling the hors d'oeuvres. It was a welcome and comforting memory.

Lena spread the oil across Ali's lips, leaned down and kissed her, then fed her another oyster and ate one herself. "Help? Yes?"

"Yes." Ali nested into the pillows, felt Dale's arm behind her head. Lena's hand stroked her belly through its satiny covering, pushing and kneading the touch-hungry flesh. Lena smelled like summer gardens back home, long ago. Ali breathed the scent in, softened into it, into her friends arms.

Tingling sensations began to spread from Ali's twat down along her legs, upward to where her breasts had once been and beyond. She took the Hatachi in her hands again and thumbed the switch.

Everything intensified.

Lena leaned over and touched her lips with the taste of oysters followed by soft lips, touching, parting, a fine hard tongue, caressing.

She felt warm hands moving along her legs, squeezing and molding her body, thawing her fear.

Ali moaned into Lena's lips. How could anyone touch her like that? How did she know just what was needed and give just that, no more?

Dale's body cradled her from behind, cradled and rocked her slightly, rocked against her.

Doors, long shut, opened inside her.

Ali rotated the Hatachi, pulsing with its insistent drone. She knew she'd have to work for this orgasm, to reach for it, to leap into it, trusting that her newest and oldest friends would hold onto her, that their loving, like a parachute, would break her fall.

Thrusting against the Hatachi, she felt the tensions building, the climax gathering. She willed herself to the brink, to finally let go, like jumping from a plane, pushing herself forward even when something in her said no, no! Bringing herself to the brink again, longing for that rush of exhilaration, the wind in her hair.

Surely letting go here was safer than the many jumps she'd made before, surely.

Dale spoke words of loving encouragement in her ear. Lena's hand kept up a slow, massaging rhythm, steady, non-obtrusive.

Mentally Ali imagined jumping. Opening herself to all her feelings, she opened her mouth to Lena's lips, her awareness to Dale's support.

She opened her spirit.

Lena's hand caressed her scars.

As Ali moved against the vibrator, her whole body seemed to go into motion. Her hips, shoulders, and head moved. Her legs and feet moved against each other. She courted pleasure, welcomed it through her skin and muscles, into her bones and psyche.

Warmth broke across her, flooding her. She felt the pain as well as the pleasure of climax, the orgasm wrenched from some tightly held knot deep inside her, spilling and flowing. She heard herself cry out as if it were a stranger's call, a strange call, yet familiar and oh, so dear. She lost herself in the soft, enveloping warmth, bathed in it, melted into it. Time passed. She relaxed and slept.

In the morning she woke to find her face pressed against Lena's chest, her hand hugging Lena to her.

"I want to make love to you," Ali said.

"Over and over," was Lena's reply. "Over and over."

The Van

I lived with Abby in San Francisco, in an apartment filled with that wonderful white light that the Bay Area is so known for: Mediterranean light some people call it.

Sex, initially, had not been easy for us. We fumbled together, never quite in sync. I might kick her in the head while changing positions or she would alter the way she was licking me and I would fail to come. I loved going down on her, but she could only orgasm through tribadism, "good old-fashioned rubbing," she would say. Often I just wanted her on her back where I could lick and touch her for hours. She said it felt humiliating. After awhile she changed her mind about that.

Things really meshed for us when she built a fold-out bed into the back of her van. It was wide enough and, with the curtains, it was very private.

The first time we took it out was in the middle of the day, one Sunday. We zipped around for a while sitting close together, then she pulled into a parking lot beside a fancy restaurant.

"I'm not dressed to go in there," I said, surveying my cutoffs.

"We're not going in, sugar," she said, climbing into the back and pulling the curtains. "Come here."

The van itself became an erotic accomplice, carrying us to campgrounds, waysides, unmetered spaces along public streets. Sometimes we would pack elaborate picnic lunches or stop at tiny corner grocery stores or produce markets, gathering, anticipating.

Abby always presided over the organizing and spreading of the meal, handling the food with the same grace she used in her professional work as a caterer.

Sometimes the food came before sex, sometimes after.

Each adventure would start with Abby's seductive, darting glance, "Want to go for a ride?"

That first time, though, I knew we were onto something hot. I climbed into the back with her, slid the final curtains behind me and stretched out beside her, fully clothed. She undid my buckle and slipped her hand inside my pants. Lightning. Hot spicy foods. Horseradish stew. Ooooo, I came so fast I didn't have time to think about it, and then I came again.

Then I pulled her on top of me and started moving in the ways I knew she liked and soon she was groaning deep down in her throat, eyes closed, rolling her head from side to side.

"Oh, my god," she said, and, "Oh, no, oh, No," and then she was grabbing me, fingers squeezing in and body rocking, legs in a scissors grip.

"Hold on, baby," I told her, "Hold on. I love you."

In the fall, after the tourists left, we'd weekend in campgrounds, by mossy rivers in the redwoods, or in gold country where the grass would be coming back after the hot dry summer. The air was crisp whenever we stuck our heads out.

We might take a break to walk the woods or beaches, bundled up, arm in arm, thankful for the cold Pacific winds that kept sightseers away.

We'd build a campfire and snuggle and romance our way through meals and coffee. She'd entertain me with stories of her adventures, her many lovers before me, the crazy ones, the fun ones. I never tired of listening. She never told the same tale twice.

Returning to the van the smell of sex would wrap around us, invitingly. We'd turn on the engine and the heater and kiss and kiss until the space was warm enough to undress in, then I would touch her for as long as she would let me, for as long as she could stand the intensity before rolling on top of me. I held her tight, curling into her, responding and supporting as she pushed and pressed against me, her neck arching up and back, incredibly beautiful.

We vacationed for two whole weeks one year, traveling south along the coast, winding, moving slowly. We made love at Big Sur with winds so strong they rocked the van, and in a secluded alcove near the Hearst castle. I came quietly on a fancy residential street in Beverly Hills before we turned east into the desert, then north, following the sunrise slopes of the Sierra Nevada.

Evenings came early. We would crash for the night and rouse with the earliest light, moving against each other, inside the double zipped sleeping bags, under the large feather comforter, knitted caps in place against the chill.

I'd get my hands under her thermal top and rub her breasts until the nipples hardened, rub and pull ever so softly. "Come here, little friends," I'd call. "Come here. Get hard for me."

She'd capture one of my legs with hers and start light humping, the steady rub, rub, rub, that would, inevitably if not quickly, bring her around.

The van was a cocoon that nurtured and protected us.

Often, during the warm middays, one of us would nap in the back while the other drove. Sometimes I'd masturbate, telling her what I planned to do, then filling in the details of spreading the hairs, moistening my fingers, reaching down. I loved forcing myself to verbalize, to externalize the activities, the sensations.

Always there would come a point where I'd have to stop talking.

"And now? What are you doing now?" she'd ask. When I wouldn't answer she would pull the van off to the side of the road and climb in the back with me, holding me, murmuring, trucks whizzing by.

On the ninth day out we had a fight, a spat really, over some trifle and, probably, our constant presence in each other's company.

"I'm just going to ignore you," she said, staring out over the wheel.

"You are, huh? Well I think I'm just going to masturbate here in the front seat beside you. A little hand crafting ought to improve my mood."

Sliding down, I propped my feet on the dash, covering my legs with a jacket, unzipping my pants and sliding my hand in against the warm, soft furs.

I wasn't sure I could come, but determination propelled me on.

She groaned.

I ignored her.

Closing my eyes, I imagined the night before, her arm around me, fingers touching me very much the same way that I was now. I heard her voice saying, "Sugar, sugar, sugar, love," and smelled that hot, sweet sexy perfume that loving draws out of our bodies.

As I touched myself I felt her arm slip around my shoulders, pulling me close, heard her voice in the present saying, "Sugar, sugar, oh sugar love."

"Tell me a story, a dirty story," I said and she told me a story about picking a woman up in a bar in Honolulu, going back to the woman's apartment and getting it on all night long.

"How did you do it?" I asked.

"With my hands," she answered. "With my hands and my whole body."

"Did you come with her?"

"I don't remember."

"Did she come with you."

"Yes, sugar, she came with me. They all came with me."

Why I found this so exciting, I can't explain, but I did. My body ached for release, ached for her hand against me. I pressed my face against her side, touching myself faster and faster, breathing faster and faster. The world around me had totally disappeared.

I found myself peaking and cresting, flying both into and out of my body, shaking and gasping and coming, coming, coming, relieved to feel close to her again.

We drove home through Reno, Tahoe, and Sacramento where we left the main highway and followed the old road that winds along the river. We both had to get back to work, but wanted to delay to the last minute. At a small delta town we found a bumper sticker that read CALIFORNIA IS WHERE IT'S AT and another that said I LOVE MY VAN.

We bought both, sticking them on the back bumper before cooking one last dinner, climbing in the back of the van, and pulling the curtains one last time—at least until next week.

Hot Sticky Sex

One luscious afternoon shortly after they had become lovers, Vi lay stretched out on the bed pressing back the damp hairs from Yvonne's cunt. The rumpled, dark green sheets testified to their hours of shared pleasure.

Sunlight warmed the room, drawing a film from their bodies, making their movements slow. It illuminated the rosy crevices before Vi, who kept saying she'd never seen anything quite like this, so many folds, layers, textures.

"You're just incredible," she said. "Fabulous. So convoluted."

Yvonne, propped against flowered pillows at the head of the bed, laughed. "I call it my yoni." She stretched and wiggled against Vi's fingers. "You know, I used to think it was so big and, well, floppy, because I'd had kids but my sister's looks the same and she's never had any."

"Your yoni, is it, pet? Is that foreign or scientific?" Vi leaned down and licked slowly from the curtained opening upward, then back down and up, circling the hard little nugget of a clit, giving it an extra flick before going down again.

"Ouuuuuuuuuuuuuuuuuuuuuuuuuuuuuu, that feeels nice." Yvonne's arms were crossed over her head, her neck extended, her mouth soft and open. "Mum, yoni, it's Indian, East Indian, but I'm not sure what language." She sighed and turned her head slowly, luxuriously from side to side.

Vi was thrilled to be in bed with Yvonne, having been excruciatingly attracted to her for months. She looked with pleasure at Yvonne's rich body, the face half turned away from her. If this was lust, she just hoped it went on and on.

Leaving her fingers inside, she glanced around the room which felt so like its owner. Sunlight glazed the philodendron leaves, rubber plants, a small banana tree. Petunias, in shades of purple and pink, bloomed in window boxes, sweetening the air. Outside, crepe myrtle's delicate, crimped blossoms echoed the fluting surrounding her fingers.

Vi blew warm air against Yvonne's cunt, licked again then pressed her whole face into those sweetly swollen lips. "I like the way you taste: cream soda with a squeeze of lime."

Shifting so she could see more clearly, she watched her thumb repeating the pattern her tongue had just been following. She glanced up at Yvonne's face. "When I was a kid I called mine my cunny." She stroked with both thumbs, adding a slow lick now and then for moisture.

"Cunny's from cuneus, latin for wedge," Yvonne said, thrusting slightly against Vi's thumbs.

"I always thought it meant cunt, like in cunty." Vi slid her first two fingers back inside Yvonne, brought the liquid out and spread it across the flowery edges, then slipped the fingers in again.

"It does. Cunt, cunny, cunty, they all come from the word for wedge. It's like cuneiform, the wedge shaped letters of the Sumerians or cunnilingus: licking the wedge. And I certainly like the way you lick my wedge, sweetheart."

Yvonne brought her arms down and squeezed her breasts between them, gorgeous breasts, voluptuous, full like her hips, like her thighs, like her mind.

Vi hummed and immersed herself in Yvonne's cunty folds. The day drew on. Yvonne came. Vi came. Yvonne came again. Long purple shadows streaked the room. Darkness gathered in the corners.

Yvonne's voice drifted to Vi from a long way off.

"You know what I've always wanted to do in bed with someone?"

"I haven't the slightest, Pet."

"I've always wanted someone to play with my ass. You know, go inside and fuck me there."

Vi hoped the twilight hid her startled look. "No, pet. I would never have guessed that."

"Interested?"

Vi was, but she was also scared. She had read about anal sex, but mostly in s/m stories, and there the context was terrifying. She didn't have a framework for imagining it in a loving setting.

"Look, I am interested and the idea does turn me on, but I have this queasy feeling about it, do you know what I mean? I'm interested, but I want to go slow and quit if it doesn't feel right."

Yvonne sighed. "My husband was a considerate lover but he thought oral sex was appalling. I never dared to mention this."

"I guess I always thought men wanted to do everything, were always looking for a woman who would open up for them."

"Well, that's not how it was with us."

"That's okay. I'm glad to be the first. Anything you want me to know about this before we start?"

"Use lots of lubrication and don't go into my cunt afterwards or I'll get a wretched yeast infection."

"Yes, I did know about not doing that. Where's some oil and a towel?"

Yvonne lit a lamp and draped a scarf over it muting the light. She lit some candles, some incense. Vi lay on the bed watching. The candlelight threw complex, overlapping shadows onto the walls. Vi thought about how complex people are, how interesting the patterns when lives overlap.

Yvonne returned from the bathroom, velour beach towel and oil in hand. "This is a first for you, too, isn't it?"

"Yes. No one has ever asked me before and maybe I wasn't ready before either." She spread the towel and Yvonne settled comfortably on it. "Do you believe that things open up for you only when you're ready? I do. I think, before that, they're just ideas, promises. Then, one day, you're ready to act on them and someone comes along saying, 'What I've always wanted is . . .' Do you know what I mean?"

"Oh, Vi, where have you been all my life?"

"Down the hall and to the left, pet." They laughed at the reference of their offices at work.

The sweet smell of the petunias mixed well with the incense which formed a faint haze in the room, an added other-worldliness. Shadows danced.

The afternoon's heat had dissipated only slightly. Their bodies seemed to cling wherever they touched.

Yvonne lay on her back with Vi beside her, massaging her bottom, working carefully along the crack, pressing and probing gently until she found the place where the flesh changed.

"Oh," Yvonne said, pressing back against her, wrapping her arms around Vi's head and drawing her tongue into her mouth.

"Oh, Vi, sweet Vi, I want you so much. Do you think this is awfully perverse?"

"Yes, awfully, and I love you for it, love you, love you."

First there was a tightness, a feeling of resistance against her finger. She paused there for a long time, waiting for the muscle to relax, feeling her connection to Yvonne intensify.

Yvonne inhaled deeply and Vi's finger slipped, almost abruptly, inside. The sensation was of a silken smoothness. She slid back and forth with ease, caressed and caressing.

Vi took one of Yvonne's breasts into her mouth and sucked. The activity seemed to calm her as it excited Yvonne, who tangled her fingers in Vi's hair.

As Vi felt Yvonne squeeze down with each inward stroke, her own muscle began to contract in sympathetic unison. She shifted so she could straddle Yvonne's leg. Softness was everywhere.

She lost herself in the rhythm of their movements, the thrusting of her finger, of her pelvis, the swaying of Yvonne's body.

Yvonne's hand slid along Vi's side, then dropped to her own crotch where Vi could feel the movements as knuckles brushed against her belly. No one had ever done this with her either. Briefly she wondered how many other firsts this relationship held. It didn't matter, though. Right now, only the moment, the movements, the radiant, explosive, all-encompassing feelings mattered.

"Don't move," Yvonne said, squeezing down so hard that Vi couldn't have moved her finger even if she'd wanted to. Yvonne squeezed and pushed, pulled and rolled against her, then cried out, shivering.

Vi rubbed her pelvis hard against Yvonne's leg, moaning and coming too, coming and collapsing and noticing the rhythmic, hard contractions, squeezing her finger. She rubbed her face into Yvonne's breast. "Love you. Love you."

Slowly Vi exited her finger. Yvonne wrapped her arms around Vi's head, kissing her and crying, her tears covering both their faces.

"Are you okay?" Vi asked.

"Am I ever," Yvonne replied.

The candles were burning low. The incense had gone out. A light, cooling breeze kissed their bodies.

Vi felt the plants as benign presences hovering at a discrete distance, purifying the air, offering blessings on this union which was starting off so comfortably, so warm and lovingly. She asked whatever spirits there were out there to help and protect them in the days and weeks and months to come.

As Yvonne lit new candles, Vi went to wash up in the bathroom. Yvonne soon followed, hugging her from behind, kissing and nibbling her shoulders.

"Maybe, next time, you'll let me do it to you."

"Maybe," Vi answered and thought that yes, maybe she would.

Raspberry Summer

The smell of raspberries always brings that summer back: raspberry jam, raspberry nectar, raspberry wine, and the sun-warmed berries pulled carefully from the bushes and crushed in my mouth.

☆ ☆ ☆

I watched Suzanne's body silhouetted against the starry sky, watched her throw herself into the dive, the awkward arch of her body, the deeper darkness between her legs.

I loved her but she didn't know, yet. She called me her special friend, her best friend, her pal. Did she even know that girls could do it together? She never talked about herself, her past. I didn't probe, just felt happy being around her.

She climbed back on the diving float and flung herself forward into another desperate dive, crashing into the water and coming up quickly, never staying under very long, gasping as her face broke water.

"You're doing fine, sport. Try to relax more. Take a deeper breath to begin with. Raise your arms more slowly, then bend."

I kept moving in the water so I wouldn't feel the chill. Suzanne dove in again then swam toward me, her teeth a pale glow in the night.

"Not very graceful, but at least it's a dive," she said, her face close. "Oh, Christie, you're so patient with me."

"You're getting there." That wild energy rose in me again, pushing me to lean forward and brush her lips, to stroke her cheek. "Race you to the shore."

Suzanne paced me all the way in, splashing a lot but keeping up. The dark mountains loomed around us. The light of the rising moon outlined their eastern tips.

I'd known Suzanne for about three weeks when she asked me to teach her how to dive. I'd loved her from the first moment I saw her. I couldn't have been happier about the lessons if I'd thought of them myself.

She arrived with the other new counselors the day before orientation, looking sort of dazed.

"Hi," I said, checking out her name tag. "Hi, Suzanne. I'm Christie. Can I help you find your way around?"

"How'd you know my name?"

"Read it," I said, nodding to her nicely rounded breasts, then feeling self-conscious as she flushed.

"I'm in "Sweet Dreams." Can you tell me which way that cabin is?"

"Can I ever. I've been coming here since I was ten. Spent my first summer in "Sweet Dreams." Been a counselor for the past two years. It's a really great place to work."

"Does it show that I've never been to camp before?" Her eyes had a hurt, pleading look, but guarded, like there were places inside her she didn't want to go.

"Sure it shows. Why didn't you ever go to camp?" I picked up her duffel and started up the path.

"My mother didn't like me to be away from her."

"How'd you get away this summer?"

"We argued until I won." She said it with a flatness that didn't invite more questions although dozens were banging around in my head. She didn't sound like she came from around here, not yankee but not southern either. Maybe one of those border states to the west. Why did she pick the Blue Ridge for her summer escape? Why did her mother hold onto her so tightly?

"Here's your cabin. I'm J.C. in the one next door. Find me if you need anything, including company."

"J.C.?"

"Junior Counselor." I settled her bag, tipped my hat and exited before I could make a fool of myself. I was smitten. So this is love, I laughed to myself, hugging her memory.

I saw her regularly, the way you do in a small, closed community. Our kids swam at the same time each morning. I'd watch her working with the beginners, little kids climbing all over her. Someone was always hanging on. She looked like she liked it.

I was stationed on the diving float with the advanced free-swim group. Sometimes I'd demonstrate fancy dives for the kids, hcping she'd be watching. I'm not much for looks but I swim and dive really well. I've a knack for it, I've been told.

By the end of the first week I'd developed a grandstand play, wanting her attention. After whistling the kids out I'd take my time doing a back flip off the low board or a triple gainer from the high.

Everyone would cheer when my head cleared the water.

Suzanne always managed to be dockside when I climbed out.

"Nice one, Christie," she'd say and touch my shoulder.

My grin would stretch my face and we'd stand eye to eye for just a moment, just a heartbeat.

She wasn't the first girl I'd fallen for, but this time I felt swept off my feet, breathless and giddy and wanting something, somehow. Something I didn't have a name for.

After one of those encounters I'd feel the touch of her hand on my shoulder the rest of the day.

One of my campers, little Liz, told me Suzanne lived down the street from her.

"Her dad shot himself, on their porch. I don't remember exactly when." Liz pushed her glasses up on her nose, her face solemn. "My mom said it was a tragedy." Liz wrapped skinny arms around herself and shivered.

I pulled Liz onto my lap to comfort her, wanting to comfort Suzanne as well. So that was part of the sadness that hung around her when she'd stare off toward the distant mountains.

Sundays were always special. We'd go to breakfast in pajamas and robes and sit wherever we wanted. I'd busy myself in the cabin until she went by, then fall in beside her.

"I have this passion for sticky buns and bacon," I'd say, thinking that my passion went much deeper.

"Yes, and hot chocolate and oatmeal cookies and wild blueberries," she'd laugh, getting to know me pretty well. Then her eyes would close over and part of her would pull away.

After breakfast we'd dress and line up for chapel, me leading my group, her shepherding hers from behind. Little Liz was usually right behind me, wrapping her arms around me whenever we stood still. Sometimes I'd touch Suzanne, but carefully, afraid somehow of scaring her away. Then we'd stand side by side, touching from shoulder to elbow as I sang hymns with more enthusiasm than I'd ever known before.

In the middle of the summer we took our day off together, packing water and lunch, climbing to the granite lookout three miles up a winding trail.

"It's so beautiful here. I wish I could stay, that life could always be like this." She spread her arms out over the expanse of blue valleys dipping off toward the Great Smoky range.

I put my arm around her waist in a gesture of comradery, but the warmth through her shirt set me tingling and I didn't know whether to take my arm away or stay.

She turned and put her arms around me and hugged tight. I savored the pale violet smell of her, the fresh soap and hot flesh smell of her. Oh Suzanne.

We stayed like that for a long time, just breathing, the sun hot, the wind ruffling my hair. When she pulled away, that hurt look came into her eyes again. She looked away and started unpacking the food.

"My father," she sighed, "well, he killed himself a few years ago." She looked at me, then away again. "He was . . . he was homosexual. He'd gotten caught and, well, my mother was going to divorce him. It was awful."

Tears came slowly down her face and her mouth quivered. I thought my heart would break for her. I didn't move.

"Did you know," I wasn't quite sure how to ask. "Did you know, that, about him before?"

"No, I heard them fighting about it, yelling about it and him saying he was sorry, that he couldn't help it. He begged her not to leave him but she wouldn't listen." She turned and looked me full in the face. "I thought I might be one too, but I don't want to be." Her eyes seemed to look right through me, to something or someone beyond.

"It may not be a choice." I kept my hands to myself, loving her, willing her to understand that our love could exist, didn't have to end in some terrible way.

She began unwrapping the sandwiches and the mood changed, the opening was gone.

Late at night I'd lie on my back in my bunk, touching myself, thinking about her. I'd imagine lying close together, pressing against her all over. One night something happened that hadn't before. I felt shaken by it, by the way my hand seemed to know what it was doing without me being in charge. I figured I must have orgasmed. I'd read about it but didn't really know what the word meant. Now I did: flying and crashing and splitting open, like so many double flips.

Toward the end of summer we climbed the trail to the lookout again, her in the lead, me behind, watching. Her legs had a fine power where they entered her shorts.

We found raspberries just before the top.

"Here," I turned to her and slipped one into her mouth, then another, resting my fingers on her lips. Her eyes were so close, her skin, the warm smell rising.

"Christie," she said, and I kissed her, knowing this was the last chance I'd have. Wanting her with all the power of stored love, a whole summer's worth of wanting and holding back.

She made a little strangled noise in her throat and put her arms around me, kissing me back, kissing me so hard I couldn't breathe, then lightening up just a bit.

"Oh, Christie, Christie," she said against my mouth and I felt something warm and wet on my cheek.

I wiped her tears and led her away from the trail, although people don't often come up here late in the season.

"Look, it's going to be okay. Not everyone's life ends like your dad's." I spread the old blanket and pulled her down beside me. The leaves made a soft padding and gave off that wonderful old forest smell.

She started pressing against me just like I'd always wanted her to, just like I'd imagined her doing. We kissed and touched and cried and rolled around and then I started touching her the way I'd been touching myself at night.

She pushed back against me, her body moving with that same kind of wanting and hunger that moved mine.

Love, love sang in my veins.

We held and touched and turned until that wonderful, flying, floating, outreaching feeling came again and again.

We never made it to the lookout that day. She slept in my arms as the sun slanted lower through the trees. When I kissed her awake she looked startled, then a slow, wondering smile started at the edges of her mouth and kept going 'til it reached her eyes.

"More raspberries?" she asked.

Kissing, Kissing, Kissing

Elizabeth lay in Carey's arms, in her lap, legs dangling over the side of the overstuffed chair. Shutters had been folded over the tall windows, blocking the cold night, the casual curiosity of neighbors. The radiator's whistle accompanied a late night country blues show. The smell of chicken soup lingered.

They were kissing, had been kissing for a long time.

Elizabeth liked kissing Carey more, it seemed to her, than she had ever liked kissing anyone. Of course it was stimulating but there was also a quality about it of good communication, like dancing with someone you care about and know well or skating, partnered, holding hands.

After two years they should know each other well. She nibbled gently on Carey's lower lip. They'd met while working on a political action campaign, side by side, doing all the tedious, necessary jobs that might add up to success. They began eating dinner together, talking, always talking. She noticed they never ran out of topics, never floundered uncomfortably, trying to find a common ground.

Carey pressed back against her mouth, her lips all soft and sensuous. What a beautiful mouth she had, finely shaped, incredibly sensitive.

The first time she'd heard Carey speak at a rally she was amazed and impressed. "You were good up there. Inspiring. I almost cried." The words seemed inadequate for what she'd experienced, the way Carey had glowed, the way her words had formed bright pictures in Elizabeth's mind.

Carey's mouth and hands now sent bright, hot ripples of pleasure across Elizabeth's body, radiant waves of pleasure that formed an amber cocoon around them, glowing.

One evening at the project office, someone had taken Elizabeth aside and told her Carey was a lesbian.

"Well, that's all right with me," she'd answered, a little too fast, a little too belligerently. She'd wondered about her fondness for Carey, the pleasure she took in her company.

Elizabeth trailed her tongue around the edges of Carey's lips, teased the corners of her mouth, slipped quickly in and out, tasting, touching.

It had taken them months to move toward any kind of intimacy, any physical touch. Elizabeth had known she was attracted to Carey, but all of her prior relationships had been with men. She felt cautious and more than a little scared. She thought that if she moved slowly and paid attention to how she was feeling, she would probably be all right.

She had moved slowly and everything had worked out better than she could have imagined.

She thought about Carey picking her up after work during those first intense months. She still held the full-time secretarial job she'd had when they met.

Carey tended bar part-time while completing a long-abandoned masters in counseling. "I want to help people," she said, "to help people who don't always have access to good therapy."

Elizabeth shifted against the chair, against Carey's legs, ran her hand through the thick curls around her ears, relaxing, kissing, glued almost together or, at least, connected by a magical bond that held them, one against the other, moving constantly if ever so slightly.

The night of the big rally, after they had all partied late, Carey had invited her to stay over at her apartment. Elizabeth had looked into Carey's eyes for what seemed like a long time, questioning, weighing her own response before saying, "Yes."

She had put on a pair of Carey's pajamas and climbed into bed, pulling the covers high, shivering with anticipation. She rubbed against Carey now, remembering the force that pulled them together that night, pulled and squeezed them together into the center of that already small bed.

Carey had lain beside her, holding her hand. It was Elizabeth who moved, her fingers seeming to have a will of their own, seeking to continue all the threads of unfinished conversation, to weave them into a larger whole encompassing what they hadn't said as well as what they had.

Carey had lain still, receptive but not moving, moaning softly now and then. Elizabeth pressed against her, slid her body along Carey's, her lips along collar bone, throat, and jaw. When she reached her lips, Carey had groaned and parted them, letting Elizabeth in, drawing her in, sucking and stroking and breathing very slowly.

Kissing had never been like this before. Elizabeth, who had not seriously considered lesbianism for herself, suddenly knew, inarguably, exquisitely, that she was one.

Kissing was all they did that night, but what kissing it was, connecting to deep, submerged levels of knowing, of loving. Warmth and excitement spread throughout her torso, tingled in her fingers and toes. There was a push and pull to the kisses, a mystery and adventure to them.

Sometimes she followed where Carey led, relaxing into the merging, flowing sensations.

Sometimes she made demands of her own, leading Carey on magical, merry chases with her lips and tongue, with the pressure of fingers against face and head, neck and ears. They would collapse against each other, laughing, out of breath with excitement.

Kissing. Would she ever tire of it? She didn't think so.

Elizabeth unbuttoned a couple of buttons on Carey's shirt, concentrating on not breaking the connection their lips were making. She slid her hand along the warm, silky skin, downward, lightly grazing the nipple with quivering fingertips.

Carey's nipple was hard. She pressed it into Elizabeth's palm. Love had a warm romance to it, a familiar flavor and odor to it. Safety and satisfaction empowered her.

Elizabeth sighed with pleasure.

They'd won the political campaign and celebrated with a pizza with everything on it. That night they made love for the first time.

Carey again lay still, letting Elizabeth roam her body, touching, holding, molding. Elizabeth relaxed into the exploration, savoring the softness, the hardness, the delicate and crisp hairs, the sweet musk of excitement. Remembering the pleasure she'd known when men went down on her, she had knelt to kiss and lick and suck that private place between Carey's legs.

"Oh, darling," Carey had said, over and over. "Oh, darling, yes."

Carey had turned and pulled Elizabeth to her, on top of her, so that she could reach her as well, doing wondrous things to her body with fingers and tongue, making her go bright and hot, making her want more.

Elizabeth followed Carey's movements, danced against them, flowed into them. She wanted the sensations to continue forever. At that point where she felt she would burst with joy, Carey's climax rolled against her. Cresting with it, she toppled into an orgasm that shocked her with its violence, with its deep, extended endurance, with its lingering afterglow.

Kissing Carey now, her lips electric, the membranes in her mouth alive to the movements of Carey's tongue, the past and present merged. Her whole body seemed erotically awake. She focused on the movements their mouths were making, their mouths and their hands. Carey tugged at the fastening on Elizabeth's pants, slipped the zipper open and her hand inside, moving down, down, acute pleasure rippling.

Elizabeth held Carey tightly to her, conscious of the moving fingers, the spreading heat. She kissed her cheek, her neck, her ear, held tightly to her breast. She knew what was coming and, knowing, expanded, reaching to her lover with more than her body, opening her mind, her joy, her spirit.

Carey's fingers brushed through her fur and found, unerringly, that point of hunger and desire. Her touch was the faintest breeze of a touch, the lightest kiss of a touch. Elizabeth ached with longing.

The radio played a sad waltz tune and she lifted her pelvis to the beat, squeezed her muscles to the beat, strained for more. Carey's fingers dipped into and out of her body, spreading warm liquid, spreading love. She pressed her face into Carey's neck praying silently for release, clutching this beloved body against her, trying to defeat the confines of space and time, the clothing between them, the separateness of their bodies.

Finally, with a feeling akin to tossing herself into the air, she danced into an intense, enveloping blueness, a radiant warmth, oblivion.

Kissing. Carey was kissing her. Carey, her own exquisite, beloved Carey. Carey with the mouth that taught her want and hunger and need and which satisfied that need as well. Carey with the dancing fingers and searching lips that never left her wanting more.

Like Deep, Fresh-Water Pools

She fell in love that autumn, but it was not an easy love, no casual affair of the senses. She fell in love, leaves turning yellow in the long, dry, cool afternoons, the light slanting through young madrone and canyon live oak. Leaves rustled under her feet like ideas shifting around in her mind, emotions wreaking havoc with her body.

This love was unasked for, unexpected, and quite exquisite.

The beloved's face hovered in her mind's eye, greeted her on waking, came to her in moments of reverie: almost tangible, touchable, incredibly present.

The sun sent out long golden rays. She walked with love, talked with love. Did not touch.

What's it like to have a dream lover who is a real person but who is not your lover, who comes to you, and with whom you come in your dreams?

Perhaps she's married or involved with someone else, or perhaps you are. She becomes your best friend but there's always something else there, this electricity between you, magnetic waves, something making you notice her no matter how crowded the room is, how compelling the others around you are.

That fall they needed rain, needed it desperately. It was the second year of too little water. Old, established trees died.

Finally the rains came. It rained for two days before she noticed, fully noticed. Her mind had been engaged elsewhere. Elsewhere in that imaginary world where they were most fully together.

First, of course, she only noticed the other, began to pay attention to what the other said, how she answered. Wanted more.

Later, who can tell exactly why or how, she wanted the other in a different way. Was it the night she learned the attraction was reciprocal? No, they seemed to have been on a collision course long before that, two moving objects following infinitely fine trajectories, drawing ever closer.

Remember, though, that they never touched.

She began to want to sit next to her, just to sit next to her. But what would happen next?

She began to dream. Of course. She would waken with the other beside her, dissolving as awareness took control.

Fragments of the dreams tugged at her throughout the day.

Then the dreams came even when she was awake.

There are some companions who offer the pleasures of the flesh or who please the intellect. This one, though, was a muse, the mind and body both cried, "Yes," both called, "Yes."

What is that deep underlying nature that can move, like a continental plate shifting, and everything that was known, was true before, must be reevaluated, relocated, reassessed? Where, indeed does love come from? How much can be traced to early images, childhood fantasies and desires, emotional connections made in that murky pre-dawn of the mind?

Along the creeks, tall cottonwoods flared early, spilling heart-shaped cadmium leaves before her.

She glowed with the after-rain radiance of autumn maple, pale and bright against the darkening fir.

The day came when she dreamed they touched each other, dreamed the other, who she now called "love", leaned forward and kissed her. She fought the dream, fought desire, tried to talk herself out of it.

The want came back.

She struggled with her senses, with her experience, with her yearnings, up and down the leaf strewn roads. The yellowing leaves had never seemed so luminescent, their deep lobes exquisitely fluted.

The want was lively in her veins.

Step by step the other leaned forward, in her mind, kissing her until her body was awash with her own desire, with her own tears.

How can I? How can I? she asked.

Please, she begged.

No, she pushed against herself.

When they were together they talked about ideas, about their lives, talked as if that other layer of existence were not real, talked as if they could be ordinary friends. Perhaps they could be in a world where everything was possible.

Sometimes as they talked, or perhaps during a pause, she would look into the other's eyes, eyes the color of deep, fresh-water pools, and she would feel the way she did when she made love.

The memory of those eyes was ever-present, sharing with her the ephemeral pink leaves of the dogwood, delicate yellow-leaved grape, sharing the winding roads and wooded slopes where late-season flowers bloomed in sunset tones or softest white. Perhaps they were the earliest flowers of the spring to come.

On one of their walks the distant mountains came into view, peaks outlined with the first snows of winter. The mountains entered her mind like a promise, glowing.

It's true they were friends, but they were not ordinary friends. They were lovers who never touched, who could never afford to touch.

"Listen," she said one evening, the moon, just past full, bright upon them. "Listen to me. I love you."

She wasn't sure that it was a good idea to say it but felt better after. They talked for a long, long time.

They had begun to make love in her dreams by the time the rains began. She walked, mist clinging to her face, walked, begging for clarity.

The only peace she found was in being thankful that the other was in her life.

☆ ☆ ☆

Years later they were talking with a mutual friend.

"We were lovers, one autumn, quite long ago now. We were lovers but we couldn't be, the situation was such. So we talked, just talked."

"Did you talk about sex, about being lovers?"

"No, not really."

"And you never touched each other?"

"That's right, we never touched." She felt herself smiling. "But, you know, I can remember every detail, the discussions we had, the way light glowed in her hair, the paths we walked, more detail, in fact, than I remember about some physical affairs."

"I think I understand."

"It was a gift, the kind that comes maybe once in a lifetime," she said, "At least nothing like it ever happened to me before, or since." She turned to the other, looked into those eyes the color of deep, fresh-water pools, and they were lovers once again.

BOOKS FROM BANNED BOOKS

Lovers,
Tee Corinne $7.95

The Assistance of Vice,
Roslyn Dane $8.95

The Contactees Die Young,
Antoinette Azolakov $8.95

Ripening,
Valerie Taylor $8.95

Profiles Encourage (Nonfiction),
Pamela S. Johnson $8.95

Like Coming Home: Coming-Out Letters (Nonfiction),
Edited by Meg Umans $7.95

Skiptrace,
Antoinette Azolakov $8.95

Cass and the Stone Butch,
Antoinette Azolakov $8.95

Dreams of the Woman Who Loved Sex,
Tee Corinne $7.95

Death Strip,
Benita Kirkland $8.95

Fairy Tales Mother Never Told You,
Benjamin Eakin $5.95

The Gay of Cooking Cookbook,
The Kitchen Fairy (distributed for Fairy Publications) $10.95

These books are available from your favorite bookstore or by mail from:

BANNED BOOKS
Number 231, P.O. Box 33280, Austin, Texas 78764

Add $1.50 postage and handling for one (1) book. For more than one book, add 10% of order total (minimum $1.50, maximum $3.00). Texas residents, please also add 8% sales tax. Send your name and address for our free current catalog and to be added to our confidential mailing list.